Echoes of Silence

Caroline Hartman

Contents

Chapter 1

N AVRIA.

The night was cold, but the heart of man colder. Decisions are never easy to make.

Maria Gonzalo, a petite blonde ,with nice blue eyes and beautiful teeth rushed out of the Masters room. She had gone into the Lady's bedroom with a plate of hot soup, to ease her fever. But she returned with a bundle wrapped up in silvery linen. She looked at the beautiful baby in it and grimaced.

Oh how she wished this was not happening, she had loved the Lady of the house but she couldn't afford to let go of a chance, to change the life of her poverty stricken family. She had been paid a humongous amount of money to steal the child and bring her straight to the shore of Navria. She remembered the damned day , she set eyes on him.

Augustus was the man behind everything. Relatively short, and plump he looked like an imp, but he never let his physical attribute deter him.

A week ago, he was given a mission, by his master. He was sent to retrieve a child, from the Marcorti household, in Navria. He didn't know what the master needed the child for but one thing he knew was that, it was no where near his damn business.

After making several trips to Navria, He concluded that he couldn't get direct access into the mansion, so he had cornered one of the maidens.

From the rose garden where he had spied Maria, he had known that she was going to fall for his trick. At first he made subtle advances towards her but she rejected, questioning who he was and what is business is. Gradually she gave him little smiles and thereafter she was putty in his hands.

Under the night sky, Maria Gonzalo moved like the Eastern breeze. She knew her life was going to end and she'd never get a chance to enjoy her wealth, if she got caught.

She cradled the child firmly to her breasts, as she raced all the while throwing quick glances over her shoulder.She ducked obstacles and jumped fallen branches, she needed to complete the delivery before anybody noticed that the baby was missing.

The soup she had left in the bedroom had a little sleeping powder thrown in it for added advantage.

As she reached the waterside she scanned the area but couldn't find Augustus, She began to shiver from the cold as a new feeling of dread, crept up her spine. Looking down at the babe she adjusted the elegant material around her small form.

She admired the tiny silver necklace around her neck, she fingered it for a while then she had let it rest on the baby's chest.Maria knew she was doing a very terrible thing, but she needed the money. She needed to show her good for nothing father that she could Make it, In this life.

Moving towards the bank she saw movement by her side, turning swiftly she faced the intruder.

He was a big man with squinty eyes and bulging biceps. Maria looked up at him as he looked down at her.She was frightened by his size, with just one fist he would squash her and bury her here in the midst of all these dirt. It was surely a horrible place to die,she thought.

The man moved one huge foot towards her, as Maria took three tiny steps backwards. Summing up courage she tilted her shin and addressed him.

"Who are you? And what is your business here"? She managed to sayalthough she was frozen inside, she really did a good job by keeping her voice steady.

The stranger looked at her hands,the bundle she was carrying moved a little . As it moved he heard the faint cry of a baby. He stretch out his hands. "I'm Argon and I've come for the child. "

Maria looked at his outstretched hands and shook her head violently."I am not giving you this child!"

Argon was confused. Wasn't she the woman he was sent to meet?. He made a move towards her, just then she turned and fled.

Chapter 2

Escape...

Running away from everything you've ever known was never easy, much more running with a child that wasn't yours, and risking everything but actually nothing.

Maria wrapped the the shawl around her mass of blonde hair which she had tied in a knot, to keep from getting in her way.

She picked up the child, whose spectacular green eyes shone with happiness from the crib.As she held her close, she felt a tug at her cloth made of cotton. Looking downward, she saw Miranda's tiny fist wrapped around the upperparts of her dress. Yes she had named her Miranda. For she was admirable by all who saw her.

Living in a small house made of plain wood in the outskirts of Town was a real struggle. The place was surrounded by dying yellowish brown coloured weeds and grass, it was the abode of grasshoppers.

During the day, the sun created a very thick atmosphere that it almost unbearable to breath and at night the remnant of the sun caused extreme heat that would always keep Maria up six times a week, trying all her best to put a red faced Miranda to sleep.

Although the place was bad enough, and the atmosphere horrid, Maria never complained.

This little house, with its squeaky doors and leaking roof tops, had once been her shield during the times that she was sought by both the authorities and her once upon a time ally. Augustus.

She smiled thinly, as she picked up Miranda's woollen cap, how foolish she had been. She sat down with the squirming baby, letting herself revel in her memories.

Past...

After her escape from the shores of Navria. She had walked miles with the child, stopping occasionally to beg travelers on the road for anything they were willing to share, ranging from food to clothing and sometimes supplies.

One fine morning, on the third day of the week, luck had shown its first smile . Maria had just woken up and was treading the long dusty road, meanwhile still trying to hide her malnourished frame slightly in the bush to avoid been seen, when an old farmer came along. He took one look at her, and bellowed.

" you shouldn't carry a fin' babe like her and allow the sun to burn her skin. Come on where you heading? "

Maria had looked at the man, smiled a little through cracked wounded lips and continued to walk. She was afraid, this wasn't a time to take to strangers. He could be a killer from Augustus end. She was a thief and a criminal, she couldn't bring herself to trust anyone.

The man waited for her response, but maria gave him the cold shoulder and moved on. Moving his carriage slowly, behind her, he took in her dirty appearance and a frown creased his forehead.

"I'm just an harmless person,I wish not to hurt you nor your child. If you don't want my help, fine, but she's going to develop a fev'er if you don get outta the sun soon."

Glancing up, Maria said. "Thank you for your generosity Mr. I'll just find a shed to rest awhile".

Ebenezer scoffed." What are you on about woman? Do you prefer your child dies than accepting help?. She slowly looked at a squirming Miranda, who was so hot, she could feel her temperature through the sheer material she'd used to wrap her up.

Sighing out of exhaustion, she slowly cleaned the sweat dripping down her neck with a little piece of fabric she'd gotten from the hem of her gown. " I have no where to go Mr, if you may, please take me wherever you go".

The following week, she had arrived in the city of Ponti. South of Navria. The city was very beautiful and its people more beautiful.

Surrounded by thick greeneries, Ponti was a sight to behold. The Women wore nice looking gowns and the men, breeches and finely sewn jackets.The people of Ponti were very hardworking, nobody wanted an aid, each tasks was done by every individual themselves.

When Maria realized that her maiden skills may not be needed in this city like she'd hoped, she had quickly chose a trade to indulge in.

At first, it was a very tedious task because she wasn't used to doing any craft back at Navria. All she did was cook,wash and clean. Gradually, making baskets didn't feel all that bad and soon, making fine baskets was her profession.

Chapter 3

As the days turned into weeks, and months into years, Maria worked hard to fend for both the child and herself. She couldn't contact any relative of hers because she knew that she'd be arrested or even dead before the letter reaches her family.

Being a fugitive was one of the hardest part of one's life. She was cautious of what she did and where she went. Several times she had tried to return the child, but all attempt was a failure, it was as if fate didn't want the child to return to its family. So Maria had taken the child as hers and had nurtured her.

On a cloudy morning, Maria had set out early to the market, she was a stickler for punctuality. As she arranged her wares on a finally decorated table, the Bayley kids rushed up to her. Looking up at them Maria smiled and said. "What can I do for you two young ladies?""We want you to solve a little problem". One of the twin said, with her hands placed on her small waist.

" Go on, ask little one?

"If you take something that isn't yours, what does that make you Maria?"

Maria was startled by the question, she hesitated for just a heartbeat. "Well children, taking what's not yours makes you ...a thief." She replied, feeling weak on her knees.

"I told you Mia!". The twin who had stood and watched the entire interaction between her sister and Maria, bounced on her heels, feeling ecstatic.

The girls thanked Maria and left her alone, she had replied with a smile on her lips. " Anytime darlings ", but deep down she could feel the deep black taste of dread rolling in the pit of her stomach. Those kids had just made her realize the gravity of her punishment. Both in heaven and here on earth.

Maria had hidden the necklace that was around Miranda's neck, the night she took her. The necklace was a half silver moon, and it was very beautiful. Several times Maria had thought of selling the heirloom in order to take proper care of the child. The girl needed the best things she could afford, but she aborts the idea almost immediately.

The necklace was the only connection Miranda had with the Marcoti family and she wouldn't take that from her too.

She had done enough harm already.

Miranda blossomed from a very happy child, to a very healthy and voluptuous woman.

Her peers snickered at her body size, yes, she was curvy in all the right places but she didn't let that deter her. She always put her hair in a braid or let it loose sometimes.

Many admired her dark chestnut hair. The girls in Town were mostly jealous of her appearance. At first, Miranda was oblivious to that fact, but as she grew older she saw the knowing looks and understood that she was different.

At an early age, she had learned how to weave baskets just like Maria. She would sit in a rocking chair at the back of the house and weave baskets till her mother would come and join her.

For dinner, they would both make pies and sometimes bake bread for breakfast. During such times, Maria would look at her, admiring her sense of maturity and beauty. Miranda, would look up at her and asked puzzled ."Mama, what is the problem? " and she would reply. "My darling, I just loved looking at you, because you make such beautiful baskets and you are such a great cook and you're very strong."Miranda would laugh, and hug her tightly.

After dinner, they would eat and sleep together in their little room, which had a licking roof, that dispersed water and a single window that didn't allow the proper flow of air.

Chapter 4

Loneliness lingers longer than companionship...

Miranda, had suggested on her twentieth birthday, that she needed her own room. And so Maria, had called a builder to extend the rooms. It was done in no time and Miranda was granted her privacy.

As she lay in her room, wearing only a sheer night gown, a candle burned by her side. Her thin mattress, had done nothing to protect her body from the harshness of the ground.Miranda welcomed the discomfort as she recounted the events of the day.

The day wasn't all that bad. She had sold an orange colored basket, which could be used for picnics or laundry or farming, or whatever it was needed for.

The lady who bought it had said it was for her daughter, and that the basket would sure complement her daughter's flaming hair.

Before the woman left she had looked at Miranda's thick curly locks and asked. "You aren't from these parts, are you?".

Miranda didn't have a response, she had blushed in embarrassment, while the woman had nodded in understanding and left.

Wasn't it weird that a 20 years old woman didn't know a thing about her history?

Since her childhood days she'd known that she was the only girl among her pairs with a different color of hair. Most of the girls had either blonde, or coal black hair. Miranda's was different.

She'd tried to ask her mother why it was so, but Maria had always feigned been too busy anytime she'd asked. Once she had asked her randomly, Maria had snapped.

" I don't want you asking me anymore questions Miranda!, aren't you satisfied with what we've got? Why do you want to dig up buried bones?"

Miranda had walked away more confused than she had been, what does she mean by *buried bones*?

She knew that she wasn't asking for too much, she just needed to know who her father was, but no productive answer was coming forth, so she had let the matter die.

As she lay in her sheer white gown, she thought about her life, and what would have become of her if she had been born in another place and time.

Would she be married? She let out a snicker at the thought of marriage. She knew most girls her age were going about searching for suitors, but she wasn't worried about that, at least not yet.

She'll only get worried when mama mentions it to her. And even still, that didn't mean she would jump into the arms of the first man she met.

That was ridiculous.

Sighing from exhaustion, she watched a fat fly buzz lazily above her head. She smiled at its stupidity, the fly was created to move around and yet this one had decided to dwell in a room that was hot like the devil's breath.

Shaking her head, she turned towards the wall, and closed her eyes, letting sleep comfort her.

Chapter 5

Miranda stood before the pantry, exasperated. Mother had told her that there was enough flour and milk to make bread, but now she stared into the empty darkness. Muttering to herself, she left the kitchen in a hurry. She picked up her white shawl and tied it around her chocolate locks, picking up her beautiful green basket, which had been woven with intrinsic designs, she set to leave for the market.

As she was about to leave through the front door, she remembered that she hadn't told her mother,that she was leaving. She turn on her heels and went straight to her mother's bedroom.

On reaching there, she saw the door slightly open. She was about to push open the door and enter, when she recalled her mother's warning, when she was five.

"Miranda dear, whenever you need me,and i am in my room, always remember to knock before entering. I do not like surprises at all they get me very jittery." Miranda knocked softly on the wooden door.

Maria who was holding a silver necklace, quickly shoved it under her bedding. She straightened up, and said softly.

"Come on in". As Miranda came into view, Maria smiled thinly at her.   " Good morning mother, how did you sleep".

Miranda, moved to adjust the blankets, as Maria tentatively eyed the spot in which she'd hidden the jewelry. "My night was a troubled one child, I'm afraid I think I've caught the flu". She sniffles mildly. Miranda moved to her side, and held her arm.

"Oh mother! I'll go get you some herbs from the market. And I'll also make some soup."   Maria smiled. "You don't have to do all that'.

" I'll do that and more. Okay! I'll see you soon, there's warm water in the hearth, if you need it".

Maria smiled and gave her a kiss on her cheeks "Thank you my dear".Miranda picked up her basket and was on her way to the market in no time.Maria looked at her disappearing form, from the window and whispered under her breath.

"You're a jewel my dear, you just don't know it. "

As Miranda neared the market, she noticed that something wasn't right, she needed to ask someone what was going on.

Looking around for any familiar face, she saw Estelle. Miranda was about to call her attention, when she stopped and took a closer look at the sight before her. It was truly hilarious.

Estelle was crouched on the ground with her backside up in the air. She was hiding behind big heavy boulders, peeping through a little opening by the side. Miranda wanted to laugh, but she held on and gingerly approached an obviously frightened Estelle.   "What in Gods name are you doing?" Miranda asked whilst amused.

Estelle turned with a yelp.   "I'm hiding from those men".Miranda looked at the uniformed men who were scouting the place and talking to some buyers and sellers.

" Those are soldiers dummy! Don't you know that?"

"I know who they are." Estelle whispered.

"Why are you even whispering?" Miranda asked puzzled.   Estelle beckoned to her to come closer. "These men are in search of a peculiar girl with green eyes. Look at my eyes! They are green, I just might be the one, so that's why I'm hiding". Miranda shook her head and laughed.

" You aren't the only girl with green eyes, there are so many other girls with such eyes around here and besides, what did you do for them to want you?".

Estelle nodded her small head like she understood what Miranda was saying.

"Oh yes, yes I know honey, that's why you better go hide those beautiful eyes of yours, just like I'm doing and I didn't do anything at all except take pa Michaels walking stick". She muttered under her breath as she returned to her crouching position.

Miranda folded her hands and rolled her eyes in defeat, the girl was not the brightest amongst the bunch. "Well, I'll see you around , just stay outta trouble! And keep that rump straight, you just might give some of the men here a wrong impression!".

She turned around and headed towards her destination, as she heard Estelle say.   "Its about time I create an impression! Don't ya think?".

Miranda shook her head and sauntered away. "Stupid girl". She said to no one's hearing.

Chapter 6

Lady Charlotte, looked down at the arriving officers from her balcony. She stood still, her intelligent eyes searching for anything unusual, but all seemed normal. Charlotte averted her gaze from the scene abruptly.

It was yet another failure, she thought.

Taking the steps firmly, her beautiful elegant gown, flowed behind her. She was a woman in her prime, every one admired her. She was strong in the eyes of the people, at least that's what they thought, but she knew deep down inside, that she was crumbling.

Approaching the soldiers, she took in the beauty of nature. It amazed her that nature which seem so perfect, could be so cruel towards her. It gave her life, and yet killed her, in return.

Waving at workers who were going about doing their various chores, she stopped in front of the commander, and said. "I trust you have news for me".The man folded his cap, that he had earlier removed from his head, due to frustration.

" Yes Lady Charlotte. I and the men scouted the Southern and Western province, i'm sorry. We didn't find her".

Charlotte looked at him critically. "Are you sure you didn't find her? You were once her lover, don't tell me you've forgotten what she looked like."

"My Lady, I'm certain. I can recognize Maria from a distance".

Charlotte smiled sweetly, but everyone present knew the smile was bitter.

" Then Raphael, I want you to find her,even if it means searching the land of the dead!

That woman stole my child, its a crime that I would never forgive nor forget! Find her and bring her here,and by God if you try as much to connive with her, to betray me, I'll make sure I find you, cut off your genital and feed them to the dogs of the street!" Charlotte gave him a daring look.

"I prom..ise to find ...her and bring her here." Raphael stuttered.

"Good. Now get your men refreshed, take as much food that you would need. I need you out of this place by dusk".

"Thank you. I'll do just that Lady Charlotte." Raphael answered uneasily.

Charlotte turned on her heels and ascended the stairs in a frenzy. She cancelled all her meetings for the day, and the next.When her husband, Christopher, came in to console her, she had pushed him away.

"You don't understand anything. You try to, but you just can't".

" She was also my daughter, you have to understand that".

Charlotte threw him a condescending look." She wasn't your daughter Chris! You can't claim a child that you never saw."

"How can you say that Charlotte? I love you."

"I met you five years after I lost my daughter, you didn't even know what she looked like. If you truly love me, then help me find her!".

Charlotte began to cry. Christopher was angry, but he couldn't leave his wife in such despair. Yes, he had met her years after she lost her daughter, he also knew that , her first husband died three months before the the child was born. Despite knowing the hurt and pain she was going through, he loved her.

Moving towards her, he raised a hand to smoothen her hair, but she moved her mass of chestnut hair, out of his reach.

Christopher knew that he had to leave her alone. He moved slowly to the door. He tried to speak to her one more time but she was already seated on her chair, facing towards the horizon.

As the door closed behind her, Charlotte let another tear drop. She was a wounded lioness, she had suffered alone for too long. It was time to make everyone feel her pain.

Chapter 7

E uphoria runs deep...

The sun was blazing hot. Insects scurried from one sloppy ground to another, trying to hide their small form, from the increasing heat.

Beautiful plants decorated the field. At one end a bunch of daffodils were surrounded by brightly coloured butterflies. The sight was enchanting.

Miranda moved quietly through the field, She was on a mission. As she touched the different herbs one after the other, feeling their texture, she visualized what it would be like to be a healer, to reach out to people and help them when they were down. Just then she found her rhapsody.

She moved with sprint, yes she would be a healer! She couldn't wait to tell mama the good news.

Maria thought it to be bad news.

"I can't let you become a healer Miranda, it's too ex-hausting".

" Ma! You can't just turn down the idea without seeing the benefit it could bring us".

"What benefit is there?, at your age you should be married, you should have had children already. Learning the rules of healing will take you awhile to digest, and you don't have time my dear".

" No mother, I want to be a healer and I'm going to become one, no matter how long it takes me!I'm a fast learner, you told me that yourself, so what are you afraid of? "

Maria was getting angry." You'll listen to me young woman!"

"I'll do no such thing Mother! I can't let you subject me to a life that I don't want right now. Please understand that I need to do this. I beg you." Miranda's voice ended with a soft note.

Maria looked at the woman that had once being a child. "Very well, if that's what you want to do with your life, then who am I to stop you?"

Miranda was overjoyed, " thank you mother, I promise to do my best, I really want this, I'm so happy".

" I believe you. You deserve happiness, tomorrow I'll take you to Lady Latisha's place, I'm sure she could squeeze in a space for you. She owes me a favor by the way".

Miranda nodded her head enthusiastically, she couldn't speak because she was afraid that if she did, mother may just change her mind.

Maria smiled thinly."Now young Lady, get going. Bring out those potatoes I bought from the market. I want to make us a splendid supper".

Miranda was curious, she placed her hands on her hips and quaked an eyebrow." What's the occasion, Ma?"

Maria smile widened. "Young lady we are celebrating you forthcoming successes".

Miranda laughed and sauntered out of the room, to get the potatoes,freshly cleaned out and ready for coo king...oh dear.

Chapter 8

New beginnings are sometimes formidable.

Lady Latisha, was a stunning woman in her forty's. She was an image of pride. She carried herself with such grace. Her hair was a thick black and her skin glittered. Her slender shoulders and tiny waist was a bonus.When younger and older women ask her how she kept fit,she'd laugh and say." It's one of the advantages of being a healer."

She was working in her little room,when she was told that Maria needed had come to see her. Latisha kept aside the herbs she was mixing and instructed that her visitor,come in.

Maria appears by the door way,wearing a green gown,and a slightly worn out sandal. Latisha smiled and stood up to greet her.

"Good morning Maria, so good to see you".

Returning the gesture, Maria said." Good morning to you too healer. I know you may be wondering why I've come ".

" Yes,indeed I am. Tell me, what can I help you with? ".

" I've come to ask you of something slightly enormous ". Maria retorted.

Latisha smiled warmly. " Do you need me to set your womb, in just the right degree? I know you may be desiring another child since Miranda has become a woman."

Maria had laughed. "That is not why I here,I assure you".

Latisha smirked and continued her teasing." Well, most women are embarrassed to talk of such matters, trust me,I know. I have worked as a healer as long ad I can remember, it is a gift that I'd love to share freely ".

Maria shook her head. "You're wrong this time Latisha. I've come to talk to you concerning my daughter. She's taken interest in herbs and would like to be a healer."

Latisha's eyes widened a notch,before she quickly his her emotion. Smiling she placed one lean hand on Maria's shoulder.

"That's is good news,so why do you look so solemn? If she wants to be a healer,then she'd be,all she needs is practice." Latisha finished with a smile that didn't quite reach her eyes.

Maria rolled her shoulder blade,making the hand that was secured on her shoulder, fall."Let's talk like women Latisha. You and I both know that she would never go far if she doesn't have a guardian."

"That is what I fear the most." Latisha replied slowly.

"Then you have to help her. I know your position and title is of importance to you. I promise you Miranda has no intention from taking that from you. She just wants to be able to reach out to the sick."

As Maria spoke, Latisha turned her back on her,she contemplated. Miranda was more beautiful than she was,with just her eyes only, she could charm her way into any heart. Her hair was a different story. If she became her guardian,then she'd risk loosing everything. She was the only great healer in these lands and be-yond, and she wasn't ready to give that up.

Making her decision she turned and faced maria.

"Bring the girl tomorrow, and tell her to find her first trial herbs in the Mangroves".

Chapter 9

Love is a flaming sword that brands its possessor.

The master sat in his inner chambers. He was a tall, rather handsome man, with a thin scar that marred his face, starting from his left eye, cutting across his nose and ending just at the start of his upper lip.As he sipped from the wine glass, he remembered how close he had come to conquering his nemesis.

He called out to the guard standing outside the door. A Navrian who had accidentally crossed borders with his, and was now paying his due. As the guard appeared at the door, Magnus took another sip from his glass, eyeing him sceptically.

" I want you to do something for me, and I want you to be discrete about it, do you understand? " "Yes master". The guard answered. " I want you to leave quietly, go to Augustus home. Do you remember Augustus?

"Yes, I do master." The guard answers with his shaven head, bowed low.

"That's perfect. What i want you to do, is take his little daughter. I want you to do all these without getting noticed, or seen. You shouldn't get caught. Do you understand? ".

"Yes master". The guard turned and left on shaky legs.

Magnus smiled softly, he loved it when he instilled fear in people.He thought of the cunning idiot, Augustus.

After the failed attempt to abduct the child of the only woman he had loved and still loved,Augustus had played the cat and mouse game with him, and he'd played it for too long. It was time to fix him.

Magnus thought of Charlotte, he could still see her smile, even if he hadn't seen her in years. Charlotte had always been a beautiful woman, she was like fire and unsuspecting men were the moth. When she turned eighteen, he had visited her father's mansion seeking her hand in marriage. Charlotte had looked at him and said words that he would never forget. "I cannot marry you Magnus Carper, you don't appeal to me."   He had left her that day with a new burning need in him, a need to bring tears to those big brown eyes of hers.

Oblivious to the fact that she had just started a war that she may end up loosing, Charlotte had watched him leave with a girlish smile on her beautiful lips.

After the incident he had left Navria and had created a little habitat for himself. Gradually different people began to join in and in no time he had his own town, which he had named Medan.

Two years later, he learned that she had gotten married to Henry Marcoti. A green eyed soldier.He wasn't mad nor jealous, he just smiled and waited for the perfect time to strike. And he knew who was going to fall first.

He remembered how angry he was when he got the news, that a common maiden had ruined his plan. Magnus was furious, he had ordered soldiers to look for her. When they had returned without the woman, he had ordered them all to be beheaded. The next day, he sent out new troops.

He was going to find that daughter of hers, and he was going to send her head of course adorned with a beautiful garland, in a box, to her beloved mother.

Chapter 10

" **M**other! I don't know what herbs to collect from there, and besides it's too dangerous, I don't want to get bitten by a snake, there are deadly snakes in there! ". Miranda whined.

" You have to do this child. If you get bitten by a snake, you'll mix an antidote in records time. I know you.Latis ha is a very difficult woman and for her to agree to teach you, you should grab that opportunity with both hands and be grateful ".

Miranda smiled softly. " Mother I know, but don't you care about my wellbeing at all? That woman is not okay in the head, only a mad person can give such an absurd quest."

Maria sighed. "I care for you more than you can ever imagine, but you need to do this. Just last week you were excited and wanted to be a healer, now where did all that excitement go young lady?".

" Don't tease me mother. I'll do it. I'll go to the mangroves immediately I finish baking the bread, and making the stew."

Maria had returned to her unfinished basket. "Do whatever you want. But don't leave this house once it is nightfall".

" okay Mama ". Miranda replied as she walked towards the kitchen.

One hour later,

"Oh my!" Miranda screamed as she saw a green snake slithering past her. She hated coming here, but she knew she had to show Latisha, that she was strong. Moving slowly and carefully, she collected leafs. She didn't know what some of them were meant for but she was going to try her best in discovering them.

By the time she was done,the sun was setting. She hurriedly retraced her footsteps, and soon, found the familiar road that led her here. She held her basket tight as she began to mix the herbs in her head.

Three weeks later, Miranda had outsmarted all the older students. She knew how to stop fevers, bleeding, stomach pains, vomiting, heal any broken part of the body.Latisha was amazed, she hadn't seen anything like this. Sometimes She'll hide and watch Miranda mix her herbs,but she couldn't find any extraordinary extract that had made her work exceptional.

Latisha knew she was treading in deep waters, but she was determined to use Miranda for her own benefit for as long as she wanted. When the time comes, She'll do what she needed to do to keep her title.She had it all planned out from the very first day Maria had come to see her.In the end Miranda would suffer so much,she'll regret the day she took interest in herbs.

Chapter 11

Augustus was sweating profusely! Out of confusion he had left his horse behind and had ran on foot, towards Magnus lair. After his daughter went missing four hours ago, Augustus and few other men had searched the whole place for her, but she had not been found. He had retreated into his room and cried bitterly. When his wife came in,she had taken one look at him an said."You are a failure Augustus!, you have brought pains into this household because of your involvement with that man!".

He had tried to talk to her,but she had shunned him. " I don't care about what you have to say,we will only talk when I carry my child in my arms". She'd ran out of the house.

As he reached Magnus abode, he asked to see him. Few minutes later,he was ushered in.Magnus stood from his desk. "Long time no see my friend".Augustus

moved and bowed before him. " good evening mas
ter".Magnus picked up his glass and tilted it towards
Augustus. "Wine?"

"No master".

" suit yourself,how have you been old friend?"

"I've been getting along just fine, until tonight."

"Oh,what is the problem". Magnus feigned ignorance.

Trying to keep his voice steady Augustus replied.

" my daughter was abducted tonight ".

" That is such a pity".

"I suppose, please Master, help me."

Magnus laughed till tears dripped from his eyes. "How
can I possibly help you Augustus?"

"You can help me by giving me back my daughter".

" I never said I had her".

"Please I beg of you, my wife will never forgive me. I'll
do anything just please let me have her."

"Well, if you're willing to do anything for that scrawny
daughter of yours, you do remember which chapter we
were,in our little secret book. Don't you?"

"I remember". Augustus answered solemnly.

" good. Now let's open that book one more time,and
this time we finish it once and for all."

Chapter 12

Lady Charlotte was having tea when Raphael returned with his men. She had offered him a cup, which he gladly accepted. It wasn't nice rejecting a gift from Charlotte. Everyone knew that.

"So tell me,what did you find out this time?"

"My Lady, I have quite some pleasing news for you."

"Go on,tell me". Charlotte said, without exhibiting any feeling.

One look at her face,and Raphael's face lost its grin. " A good source of mine,told me that Maria lives in Ponti ". He looked hopefully at Charlotte.

She took another sip of her tea and savored the taste. She wasn't feeling excited, she'd never allow herself to feel,until the day she'd see her daughter in the flesh. " Is your source credible? "

"Very credible my Lady".

" Send for them, I want to speak with your source."

"My Lady! That's quite extreme. Sources never expose themselves. It's very risky".

" I don't intend to see their face. Don't get me wrong, I said speak and not glare. So send for them, I need to get answers, private ones."

"I'll do just that my Lady". Raphael replied defeated.

Charlotte poured fresh tea,into her now empty cup. " you may leave".

After the meeting,Charlotte had attended to other activities. She was a wealthy woman,and that called for a strong hand. If she didn't run her household with an iron fist, she was afraid it would end up in rumbles

The first place she visited was the laundry room. She stood silently at the back of the room and watched as the ladies did the laundry diligently. She smiled at a few as she made her way to the kitchen area.

The kitchen was big,with various utensils stacked up in different positions. The floor was polished clean, and the windows cleaned to perfection. Charlotte watched the young maidens, as she stood there she remembered that Maria Gonzalo, had worked in this same gro und.She wondered how someone who had been trusted enough to work in the kitchen area, could go behind her back and commit such an atrocity. Charlotte looked at the faces of all the women as they went about mixing different spice and food items, all she saw was Maria's face. She decided to skip lunch.

Moving to the labourers,she noticed they were tired. She told them that lunch would be ready soon and they should go clean up before it was served. They all thanked her.

Returning to her room,she sat on her soft bed which was covered with purple blankets, and wondered if her daughter had even eaten breakfast.

Chapter 13

Hope...

Raphael's trusted source reached Navria three days later. Charlotte had asked her servants to attend to them discreetly. After they have had their rest,Charlotte asked Raphael to bring them into her office.

Sitting in her study she backed the door as the source sat in the opposite chair. Charlotte folded her hands and said. "Good afternoon whoever you are".

" Good day to you too".The gruff voice that came from behind her,startled Charlotte a little.

"I trust you're well rested, and ready for my questions".

" yes,I can provide you with useful information. I know I'm not suppose to ask you this,but what would you need her for".

Charlotte moved to the window and placed her hand softly on the plane. "What I need the information for,is none of your business. I trust you know where you are?"

"I'm sorry for been too inquisitive."

"Well I guess that's what you're best at".

" I do mind my business almost all the time."

"Good, I do not want any part of this meeting getting into another ear".

" I'll do well to remember that".

Charlotte closed her eyes and took in a deep breath. It was time for her to find out the truth. "Tell me, I'll like to know how you knew Maria Gonzalo"

"Maria is a very successful woman,a good number of people know her."

Charlotte interest was piqued, she moved slightly to her left. "What made her so successful, if I may ask.".

" Maria is a good Craft's woman,one of the best I've ever seen."

On hearing that Charlotte restrained herself from facing the voice behind her. "What do you mean by crafts woman?"

"She was very good at making baskets, and beautiful ones too."

"Hmmm,are you sure of this?"

"Yes"

"So is she married?"

"No,she had stayed single and had raised her only daughter herself."

Charlotte frowned a little. So Maria had the effrontery to keep her away from her child for this long.

"What does her daughter look like?"

The man smiled. "She has dark chestnut hair, just like yours and beautiful green eye"

Charlotte's eyes widened in recognition. Those eyes and hair. Was really her little one.? "You said she is pretty?"

"She's stunning".

" does she wear jewelries? " Charlotte asked hopefully.

"None that I've seen her with". The man replied.

Charlotte's excitement died down a notch. " That's all the questions I have for you, when you return to your room,I'll send Raphael to you".

"Its was a pleasure doing business with you".

Charlotte didn't reply. She heard the door close behind her, turning quietly, she sat on her chair. So it was true. Her daughter had been in Ponti all these time. Getting her strength back she went back to her room, a little smile playing on her lips.

The next day, the man returned to Ponti with a bag full of gold.

Chapter 14

Miranda was like an eagle soaring in the wind. Everyday she made new discoveries and gradually news began to spread that another Latisha was blooming. Latisha smiled at all the comments but her heart was hard as stone. Nobody compares to her.

Miranda,treated every patient that came to Latisha's domain, not because she wanted to, but because the patients had admitted that, they felt more safe in her hands. The other girls grew jealous overtime, but none could confront her,because of the golden rule.One particular girl stood out from the others. She would always look at Miranda admiring as she worked. Her name was Lucy.

Lucy was a smallish blonde ,with big blue eyes that made her eyes,look too big for her face.

One morning , Miranda was cleaning a cut that a man had incurred by sheer foolishness, when Lucy had sat beside her,and help her cover the cut. After that day the two became inseparable.

They fetched herbs together and talked about everything. Lucy had revealed to her that she was not from Ponti, but had grown up here because her mother had moved after her father, ran away from home. Miranda didn't have much to tell her. The little she knew was all she could share.

Lucy was watering the locally grown herbs in Lady Latisha's garden,when Isabel, one of the girls in training had approached and addressed her rather saucily. "So I see you and Miranda are now buddies".

" what do you want Isabel? "

"I don't want anything from you Lucy, you've got nothing to offer."

"Then stay away from me you pest!"

"Oh-ooh, am I making you anxious? Don't worry Darling, I won't bite". She made an extra exaggeration by biting her teeth.

Lucy looked at her, with eyes full of amusement. " I'm not scared of you, you silly girl".

"Of course, you wouldn't. Why should you,when your friends a witch!". Isabel snapped.

Lucy had made a move to hit her,when Latisha called from inside." you two,come inside this minute! "

They had both walked in with their faces down. Latisha made a rule that no one should exchange angry words with another. She had elaborated, that as a healer one should talk less and worked more.The punishment for this act was twenty lashing, before an audience.

Chapter 15

Augustus was ecstatic. After so much time he had finally found the answers he'd been looking for. He couldn't wait to tell Magnus, he knew that Magnus had waited a long time for this.

He asked the guard on duty to inform Magnus of his presence. Five minutes later,the guard returned.

"I'm sorry,but the master demands that he be left alone".

" what do you mean? Did you tell him that I Augustus wants to see him?"

"Yes". The guard had answers with finality.

Augustus nodded at the guard as he turned and left the room. On his way home he thought of the agreement he had with Magnus. Would Magnus really turn him away? What was the reason behind it?

Too drawn into his soliloquising, he found his feet leading him to a brothel. He took one look at the place, seeing the broken down building and its occupants made him feel nauseous. He had never been in a brothel before and visiting one, is certainly not what he wanted right now.

He turned his tired feet, back towards the direction he had come from. He had moved several feet from the place, when a beautiful voice called out. Augustus wasn't one you could easily charm, but the voice kept on ringing in his ears.

Turning around,he saw a very beautiful girl, she was standing at the front of the building and was engaged in a heated conversation with an older man, who looked drunk and ready to collapse.

Augustus thought of ignoring the scene before him, and just go home. But on a second thought, what was he going home to?His wife had not returned since the day she ran away. His daughter had not yet been found. He was a lonely man.

Moving over,he saw that the girl was really angry and the man in question was sleeping while standing. Augustus approached the girl with care and chose his words carefully.   "What seem to be the problem lady ?".The girl eyed him. " Who are you? And what is your business here?"   "I'm just a passerby. The man you're talking to is obviously asleep, why don't t you let him go".

" Are you willing to pay me what he owes me?"   "What?" Augustus asked perplexed.

"You heard me the first time,now if you don't mind, excuse me". The girl turned and left, haughtily.

Oblivious to his surrounding, Augustus went after her, as he entered the parlor, he noticed the place was filled with men. He looked around for the woman who he'd earlier talked to,but he couldn't find her.

He wanted to sit and wait for her to return. Perhaps she was the bar woman, and she had gone to the back to take a leak. But his tired limbs were saying a different story. Making up his mind to leave,he pushed open the door, and the last thing he saw was the mouth of a gun pointed at him.

Augustus died before his body had hit the ground. He bled all he had, on the brothel floor...

When Magnus heard the news,he looked up at the night sky and said.

" You my friend was a good man. I'm not sorry I ended your life, I couldn't let you end mine first.Do not worry about your daughter, she'll always remember you as a lying, cheating, thief. At least that what I'd tell her you were.Now rest on friend".

Chapter 16

Freedom...

Argon couldn't believe his luck! The gods were really by his side. No one enters the den of Magnus and comes out alive. He smirked and looked at his un-bounded wrist. He was a free man once more. Taken a huge step out of his prison room,he smelled the air and looking towards the sky,he smiled.

Magnus had given him two options, find the girl and find the girl. At that time he was too shaken to even comprehend what was been said to him, he had fell in one knee and proclaimed his total loyalty. Now as he stood, he realized that he didn't know where to start searching. He needed to embark on the mission, but first he needed a strong ale and possibly a soft willing woman by his side, to keep him company all night.Its been too long.

Finding a drink was much easier then finding a woman. All the ladies that he'd approached, were either too dumb or too coy. Walking towards a brothel, he pushed open the entrance door and stumbled in, liquor in hand. Glancing around the room, he saw blurred faces of men and women, he moved his heavy form and collapsed on an rickety chair.

Bianca saw the beast of a man collapse on the half bent chair, she had almost let out a scream when his weight visited the chair, but she had relaxed when noth-ing happened. Looking into the eyes of the man she was with, she whispered softly into his ears, and the man's eyes lit up in surprise. In no time he made his way upstairs, with gaiety..

Looking across the room, Argon, saw the redhead beauty whisper into the ears of the man she was with, her corset tight enough to strangle a man. Taking the bottle to his lips he took a gulp and let some drib-ble down his chin. She was that breathtaking.avertin g his gaze from her luscious form, he concluded that there was no point in ogling another mans property. His thoughts were interrupted as a soft voice spoke from the right direction.Turning his head, he saw her staring at him, with a thin smile gracing her lips. "I said,you look lonely, from the way back." She repeated.

"Oh, I.. Yes. I came alone." He replied breathlessly.

"That is quite unfortunate, at this time of the year, one shouldn't be lonely".

" what time of the year is it?" Argon inquired.Looking at him strangely. Bianca sat at the opposite chair. "Its the period of ilutium, where people make new friends, and lovers unite" she looked up at him, and caught just the tiniest glimpse of confusion in his eyes, before he quickly masked it. "Who are you? Where have you been all these years?". Bianca asked, eyes wide.

Chapter 17

The greatest medicine to heal any heart is love.

Lady Charlotte, stood in front of the elegant bronze mirror, it had been a gift from Christopher, he was a stickler for shiny things.

Inspecting her transformation, dressed in a common peasant clothing, comprising of a brown tattered gown to worn out sandals that had some of its straps missing. Her hair had been styled haphazardly by her maid, Violet, and her hands were encased with cheap jewelry.

She was satisfied with what she saw, she could hardly recognize herself, as she moved around in front of the mirror.

Taking a quick step, she faced Violet who was standing idly, at a corner. "I want you to pack up four to five days journey worth of food and less expensive clothes, I want everything to be ready before night fall."

Violet looked at her in apprehension. "Yes my Lady" she was hesitant, "I'll do as you've instructed me" . Moving towards the bedroom door, Charlotte's voice stopped her from leaving.

"Do you have anything to tell me Violet? You can say it now."

"Yes My Lady, I think it will be a good idea, if you let the men go. You're a Lady, you aren't even suppose to wear those." Violet gestured by pointing towards the attire. "I mean they're not fit for you my Lady. "

Charlotte looked at Violet's small tender form. she picked up a hairpin from her table as she asked. "How old are you violet?"

Violet wasn't expecting that kind of question, but she answered. "Twenty and two my Lady."

Charlotte smiled. "That's why you'll never understand any of the actions I take.I was your age when I had my daughter, although I was a mother, I was too naive. I let my child grow up in a foreign land, eat foreign foods, wear foreign clothes, all because I let myself believe that, they'd find her and bring her to me."

She looked at Violet, whose eyes shown with sympathy.

" its time I go out there and find her myself". Charlotte adjusted her hair as little strands escaped from the band. "Make the necessary preparations that I've asked of you Violet. Do not be worried about me, I know just where to go."

Chapter 18

Determination bores both bitter and sweet fruits.

From the back of the house, Maria listened for sounds of footsteps but heard nothing. She had woken up quite early to start weaving up a basket that would fetch her a good some of money, when she'd knocked at Miranda's door and got no response. She suspected she was still asleep and had left to do her business.

But two hours later, Miranda was still not out. Pushing open the room door, she was greeted by a strong stench coming from Miranda's healing supplies. Her curiosity got to her,and soon she was rummaging through her things, only to find a thin bottle oozing with strong odour. Maria had replaced her find, and had left the room quietly.

As she placed the last straw that completed the bas-ket, she heard shuffling at the front door. She hurriedly moved to the kitchen and waited for the intruder to venture in.

Miranda was so tired, she felt faint. So she had taken a spot under an almond tree, to rest for a while.

When she was younger, she'd come here and just sit till night fall. The vies was spectacular, from here she could see their little house and all the way to their kitchen was visible. As she placed her back on the tree,movements from her house caught her attention. Startled she turned to see what it was, Mama was supposed to be at the market at this time,she thought.

She stood up from the spot and squinted her eyes to see clearly, the intruder was definitely not mama's. Before she could stop herself, she sprinted half way through the yard and then stopped abruptly.

Taking another route, she came through the back of the house. Taking the kitchen door, she quietly entered and as she closed it , a loud bang behind her, got her jumping high in the air, she turned. "Mother!," she said in an alarmed hushed tone.   Maria moved towards her with open arms, "I've been waiting for you all morning! Where have you been? Someone's at the front door, so no talking!". Miranda pressed on. " Who do you think it is?"

Maria looked at her. "How am I supposed to know?" She replied confused.

Miranda picked a spatula from its position at the left corner of the kitchen. She whispered. "Mother, I'll go out there and find out who it is, you stay here. I'll be back".

Maria pulled her back. "What are you trying to do? You can't go out there,what if they are here to hurt us.?"

"No one will hurt me. I have my weapon " she took one appraising look at the spatula.M

aria tried to discourage her, but Miranda opened the door leading to the living room, and stepped out.

She took in the state of the room, it looked untouched. She moved stealthy towards the bedrooms. Mother's room had been untouched just like the living room, but hers was a different story. It looked like a war had taken place. Everything thing was torn apart, her room had been ransacked thoroughly, all her healing herbs, were gone, her newest discovery taken.Miranda screamed.

Chapter 19

"**I**n us lies the seed of wisdom."

Squeezing the dry weed with all her might, she could feel its little twigs bite into her flesh. She hoped that a tiny bit of liquid would come out. But like the previously discarded plants scattered on the ground, it was yet another failed attempt. The leaf was dead.

Sighing out of exhaustion and anger, she threw the weed down in desperation. She couldn't get anything right. Since the day her elixir was stollen, she had been in disarray.

Picking up her dress, she matched like a horse in battle field, she crossed the Garden in no time.

Moving into the inner room quickly to avoid been seen, a greasy voice stopped her on her track.

"Where are you going? Latisha asked, as she moved towards Miranda, swaying her hips, in an elegant white dress, with gold embroidery on its edges.

" Good morning my Lady". Miranda greeted with her head bowed, and hands nicely folded behind her.

"Save your greeting before i strike you!I believe I asked you a question?". Latisha warned, with damning look in her eyes.

As perplexed as she was Miranda replied politely. " I was heading inside to collect one of my healing herbs. I was thinking I could use some......" Lady Latisha didn't wait to hear all of it.

"Hold it young woman! I made it crystal clear to you and all the other girls, that evey herb you mix here, automatically becomes mine! You can't take anything from Here!" Latisha screeched.

"I'm sorry Lady Latisha, I promise it would never happen again". Miranda spoke quietly.

" Better doesn't. If I find out that you go against my rules, I'll make sure you leave this place without finishing your training.

"Now leave my sight! Latisha shouted, as she pointed at the door.

Miranda left, not quite understanding why Lady Latisha, had reacted that way to a harmless attempt she had made.

As Latisha watched her leave, she moved to her inner room and unlocked her safe. It had been the one and only gift her miserable father had given her, in his entire existence.

It was falling apart, but she wouldn't dare discard of it, she didn't want his rotted skeletal being bothering her in her sleep, ever again. She needed her beauty sleep and no one was going to take it from her, not even ghosts from her part.

She removed the clear liquid, with its pungent smell. Holding it she held her breath and tried not to puke. She didn't know what the mixture was for, but she had a nagging feeling that it was not yet at its final stage.

She almost knocked it down out of anger, but restrained herself at the last minute. She needed to discover what it was, but how? That was the question.

2 Day's later

Miranda was sulking, Maria had noticed. She was a happy girl and for her to feel sad, something serious must have gotten to her.

"Hello mother". Miranda greeted absentmindedly, while twirling a blue coloured ribbon.

Maria felt a pang of guilt. " Hello child .You didn't go for training today. I know something has been bothering you, what is it?

Miranda turned big green eyes at Maria. "Its nothing serious mother, you don't have to worry."

"It is everything to worry about my dear. You rarely feel this way.Once when you were a little girl, you got moody and when I asked, you said your little friend, a lizard, you found in the woods died that morning."

Miranda smiled, and it warmed Maria's heart.

she let out a slow breath. "Okay mother, remember that Pungent mixture you saw in my room the other day?'

" yes I do"

"I have the feeling that I was doing something so great, I know somehow that that herb would have saved so many lives, somehow. Now its all gone." She let the ribbon fall from her delicate fingers.

"Miranda, listen to me. You started that mixture alone didn't you?" Maria asked.

"Yes mother"

"Then you can do it all over again my dear".

" Can I? I'm really afraid. I didn't know what I was doing the first time, mother. Miranda cringed.

Maria looked at her with a bright smile. "This time you will".

Chapter 20

We make a road when there seem to be none.

As she hid behind an oak tree, the wind blew with so much ferocity, Charlotte felt the chill and took a look at her torn and dirty dress.

She could hear the sound of the horses approaching, from behind, and quickly straightened her aching form.

The hooves of the horses got louder and so did her heart beat. She held on tight not wanting to give the riders any clue of her position, she was determined to out wit these men.

One week ago

A day after she left Navria, she had sensed the tension in the air and knew that something wasn't right. She pushed the feeling away and continued her journey.

As she traveled the stony part, she let out a breath of relieve. Finally she could see where she was going!

Enough with the leaves and shrubs. It had taken her two days to leave the forest. She would never forget those nights as long as she lived.

Her excitement was cut short when the outline of a horse appeared from a distance. Charlotte's first reaction was to turn back and head the way she had come, but looking closely around her she realised with dread that she was surrounded.

A man who appeared to be the leader of the group, had approached her, with hands stretched up high, in an inviting manner.

Charlotte looked at his short form.He was chewing on a stick with his broken browny teeth. His head was shaven to the skull and at the side of his neck was a branded snake tattoo.It was no mark she recognized.

As she observed her opponents, she concluded that she could easily deal with the issue at hand or out run these men.

Her horse was not the best, but it was the fastest amongst all, she cringed when she saw that they were armed. Her greatest fear was their weapons.

Beady black iris, started at her, arms still open wide. Charlotte looked at him quizzically.

She straightened her spine, and her voice laced with authority, she asked. "Who are you?

The man a little bit startled by her courage, gave a quick glance at his gang members, who were slowly closing in on the two.

His men chanted strange names that Charlotte couldn't understand. It was like a sort of praise, the man in question swelled with pride and then he answered, puckishly." I am Zoak, I own these lands".

Charlotte didn't have the time for such nonsense conversation with thieves. She had a very important mission before her. But she knew that her only chance of getting out of here untouched was slim. She decided to play his game, and beat him at it.

Smiling, Charlotte gently placed her arm of his shoulder. "Hello Zoak, I must say, your land is quite big."

Zoak, was momentarily taken aback by her calmness. He took one look at the hand on his shoulder and began to feel stirring in his loins.

The feeling of her soft hand on him was indescribable.

It had been a long time since a lady willingly touched him!

"What are you do..ing? He managed to ask.

Charlotte feigned ignorance, and swiftly removed her hand. " I'm sorry, did I hurt you?

"No, but don't touch me again!" He said fiercely.

"I won't. I'll be on my way now. Zoak. Thanks for stopping by." She held her rein tightly.

Seeing no kind of threat, she stirred the horse. As she moved forward, the men who had gathered around her moved away. She was frightened but she didn't look back.

She couldn't look back, if she did she was sure he would stop her, and that would be her doom.

Zoak looked on as the lady rode away. His men threw confused glances at him. But he was powerless for she had charmed him. He watched till she was out of sight.

Later that night Zoak and his men rode their horses in search of her.

Present

As Charlotte rested at the foot of the tree, she tried to keep her weary eyes open.

She would have been in Ponti, and probably have her daughter in her arms, if Zoak and his foolish men hadn't come after her.

Moving to her right she checked for them and saw that they'd once more taken the wrong part. Idiots. She muttered.

Picking her self from the ground carefully, her thin bracelet fell of her wrist, but she was too tired to care.

She carried the bag that contained just one finger of banana, and stale bread. Looking up at the brewing storm, she continued her journey.

Chapter 21

Terror lies in the heart of every man.

The sky was thick with black clouds, the wind pushed angrily at the trees, and birds flapped their wings with urgency as they flew with the strong wind, trying to find their way home.

Despite the chaos, Argon felt like a new man. He was rejuvenated, Bianca had done a good job. He hadn't felt this good in a long time.

Hell it has really been a long time.

Looking up at the sky , with his left hand shading his eyes from the dirt and debris flying around. He dropped his tattered bag at his feet, he needed food and clean water before the rain comes.

Moving his heavy form, he went in search of meat. It was easy to find one owing to the frenzy of the animals.

An hour later, with the increasing tempo of the wind, Argon held a dead bird in his left hand.

Placing the bird on the ground, he went ahead to pick up as many wood that he would need for preparing the meat and keeping warm, during the night.

As he stretch to carry another chunk of wood,he saw a thin shiny thing on the ground.

Reaching for it, he place the thin object on his palm. He wouldn't have noticed anything suspicious about the object, but something piqued his curiosity.It was too clean. He rubbed his thumb around the edges, as he wondered.. Has someone passed through here? Surely this route was not for the usual travellers.

He put the piece of jewelry in his breeches. Maybe when he goes back to town he would give it to Bianca. It would look beautiful on her delicate arm.

Several hours later, the sky began to weep. The drops hitting the ground and pushing out the earth with its force. Argon sat like a brick in the small cave that he'd managed to secure, just before the rain hit the ground.

He put the last piece of meat in his mouth as he thought about his target and how he was going to accomplish his mission.

Ponti was three days away, but with this weather it would take a week to get there.

He let his back rest on the wall of the cave. Closing his eyes, he welcomed the cool calm breeze that kissed his being.

Chapter 22

Miranda couldn't stop smiling, she'd done it. Through the help and support of her mother. She tied her wavy hair tightly in a bun. Moving around the room, she tried to keep her excitement in check but couldn't."Mother!" She called out with an excited voice.

"Stop screaming Miranda! What has gotten into you". Maria rushed in, looking startled.

" Mother I finally did it!, I've made something extraordinary and I know it!". Miranda continued speaking excitedly.

Maria tried to understand, but was obviously failing at it." What did you do? Stop keeping me in suspense!" She snapped.

Miranda let herself cool down a bit. " I have completed the herbs, I added Rosemary to enhance its fragrance. Mother it smells so good now! You don't have to squeeze your beautiful face anymore". She finished with a smile.

"That is great news, my dear. When would you show it to Lady Latisha?" Maria asked, as she beamed with admiration.

Miranda, sighed as she answered. " I'll take it to her tomorrow morning. I know she'd be so happy." Her face lost its smile.

"Yes, I know she would be proud of you. Why do you look like that?"

"Mother, something's been bothering me." Miranda spoke softly ad she meticulously weaves her hair, out of habit, whenever she was nervous.

"What is wrong? you can talk to me my dear".

"Lady Latisha, never allows us to use any herbs we make. I know she owns everything we do, but she shouldn't take all the glory.". An upset Miranda moved over to the window.

Maria smiled softly, and went over to her to pat her hair, which was completed. " My young one, I know you feel that you need to take a little credit for what you've done, but trust me a time will come when you'll take all the credit. Not just a little."

"Mother, if only she treats us like human beings, I wouldn't complain. She's so authoritative and unkind. Herbs and her attitude do not sit well. I wonder what she does in that little room, she's always in." Miranda finished with a huff.

Maria started to reply, when they both heard a knock at the door. She went to answer it, all the way wondering who it might be, she wasn't expecting anyone at this time of the day. All her baskets had been delivered to their appropriate owners.

She opened the door and saw Lucy, Miranda's friend. Maria had met the girl once at the market and had the conviction that she was a good child.

Smiling brightly, she opened the door wider for her to come in. " Ah! Lucy, what a surprise to see you! How are you child?"

Lucy bounced on her feet as if she couldn't wait to leave. Apparently, she was fidgety and Maria noticed. "I'm doing all good. Thank you Mother. Please can I see Miranda? It's urgent." She attempted to smile, but it ended up looking all wrong.

Maria frowned a little at the urgency she heard in her voice. "She's right in the kitchen Lucy. I hope all is fine?"

Lucy moved quickly to the kitchen, sparing just the briefest of glance at maria. "Everything's fine. Lady Latisha just needs Miranda back at the healing house, its nothing serious. You don't have to worry."

Maria let out a breath of relief . "oh that's fine, hurry up, she's in the kitchen!" She replied, but Lucy was already gone.

Miranda was cutting the vegetables when Lucy appeared looking all worried. She stopped cutting and looked at her enquiringly. "What is wrong with you Lucy? Do you know you could give someone an heart attack with that kind of look!" She said, as she dropped her knife on the makeshift counter.

Lucy sauntered over. "I'm sorry for causing such fright, but lady Latisha is asking for you."

Miranda squeezed her forehead in a frown. "What does she need me for? She knows I'm off today. What could she possibly need? A massage?"

Lucy threw her hands up in exasperation. "I don't know, but I'm sure this is not a time be sarcastic, you're not too busy to save a life I hope? Because it looks like that's what it is all about."

"Fine, I'll go with you, I don't want to get blamed for anything. Just wait awhile, I'll put all these back in pla ce".Miranda finished with a sigh, as she moved about putting the items she was using back into their shelf. She placed the potatoes and carrots in a bowl, and covered them neatly.

Few minutes later, Miranda and Lucy dashed out of the house. Maria who had been in her room, sewing a dress, looked out the window and smiled.

Miranda hurried towards the part that led to the healing house. Her newest discovery sat idle on the kitchen table, untouched...

Chapter 23

Lady Charlotte wobbled as fast as her tired legs could carry her. She wrapped a thin material around her head to protect her from the stinging sun. She was very tired, but the thought of finding her daughter was her strength. Lifting the material that had cascaded from her head, she put it back in place.

She took another step, and her stomach rumbled. She was famished. After her encounter with those thieves, she'd lost most of her supplies, she hadn't thought much about it at first because she had been running for her life, but now she prayed to find anything eatable.

As she stood in disarray, she heard the faint sound of drumming. Moving her tired feet, she was determined to find the source of the sound.

Climbing a steep, she saw what she had been look-ing for. Ponti. A lone tear escaped from her eye her daughter was somewhere down there. The feeling was indescribable.

Climbing down steadily, Charlotte lifted her dirty dress to ease her movements, and held on to the cloak which hid her form.She Approaching the main square, a young woman in a green gown visibly cringed, at her attire. Charlotte sent her a reassuring smile, but the woman picked up her little daughter and moved out of sight.

Smiling thinly, she took another look at her dress which was barely intact. She looked like someone who had just fought her way out of the lion's den, She wouldn't blame anyone who couldn't stand her presence.

At the far right of the main square stood an older man. Charlotte had noticed his stare but did not pay any much attention, as he stole one more glance at her. Charlotte moved towards his direction if anyone could help her, it should be him.

The old man picked up a necklace from a little table in which wares were displayed to catch the attention of buyers. He pretended to examine its beauty, but he knew that the woman with the cloak around her, had noticed him and was coming towards him at a steady pace.

Charlotte reached the old man, feeling out of place she kept both hands by her side and smiled pleasantly.

"Good day Sire." She said, her voice suddenly filled with uncertainty.

The man dropped the necklace, turning around slowly he picked up his fray stick. "Good day, how can I help you woman? Do you need something?"

"Well, I just want to ask some questions. I don't want anything, but I assure you, your wares are beautiful." Charlotte said in a hurry.

The old man heard the urgency in her voice. Taking his seat, he looked up with eyes full of wisdom. "I'm old, but I know that a woman of your status shouldn't be here. It is too dangerous. What can I help you with?"

Charlotte was taken aback by his recognition, she looked around and let herself relax when she saw that no one was within hearing range. Moving closer, she whispered. "My name is Charlotte and I seek a woman named Maria Gonzalo".

Chapter 24

Shaking her head frantically, she couldn't believe it, wouldn't accept it, he couldn't be dead. No!She placed her head steadily on his chest again checking for the normal *thud thud rhythm of a heartbeat, but like the first time, she heard nothing.Miranda looked with horror at the ashen face of the man she had been attending to for the past hours, he looked like death itself. But she couldn't bring herself to believe it.

Standing up like the speed of light, Miranda moved to the end of the tiny room. Her heart beating wildly. What had just happened? She looked at her hands which were shaking terribly. Had she just killed a man?

Her whole form shaking from fear, she moved to her medicine cabinet and took a close look at all the herbs she had in store. Nothing was out of place and yet a dead man was lying a few feet away from her.

Miranda carried on, looking and smelling them one after the other, she had made them with her own hands, and had always took pride in doing a good job. She was confident and sure that nothing would go wrong.

But yet she looked at the still form of the man. Unmoving, cold. Miranda let the first tear drop, she slid unto the floor as she cried. What was she going to do? Who should she tell? Even if she told someone, would they believe her? She was sure that the people of Ponti would hang her without even giving her a proper judgement. Death had never been taken lightly by the villagers and she wasn't expecting them to understand a word of what she would say. That's if they even let her speak.

Standing up from the ground, feeling dejected and lost, Miranda moved closer to the body. She didn't know what to do so she placed a soft blanket over it. Putting both hands together and sniffing quietly, she said a prayer. Today she could die or she would stay alive, but one thing was certain she would have to determine which she wanted.

Moving over to the door, she turned and took one last look at the man's body, she knew he couldn't hear her, but she couldn't stop herself from whispering the words, "I'm sorry". She truly was sorry for ending his life, even though she still didn't understand what had just happened.

As she ran out of the door, a lone figure who had been watching from the window, turned and left with a satisfied smile gracing it's lips.

Miranda never stopped for once, she ran all the way home. She wasn't so much afraid of her fate, she was more afraid for her loved one, Mother.Her mother would understand, she was sure.

Approaching the house, she slowed down a little, her legs were burning from exhaustion but she didn't care. Her chest heaved and her throat felt dry and patchy.

Miranda felt a sense of security wash over her as she pushed open the door. She didn't wait for the door to close as she shouted out for her mother, " Mother!, mother where are you? Moth.."

Maria who was at the backyard weaving a purple coloured basket when she heard Miranda's teary voice, flung her basket and dashed toward the open door leading to the little sitting room they had.

As she appeared at the door, Miranda who was coming out from the adjacent room was about to call out again, when she stopped her, "what is the screaming all about my dear? I've told you to not come in screaming like that." She took a closer look at Miranda's disheveled form, " What happened? why are you crying?

Miranda only sniffles harder at Maria's inquiry gaze.

" Mother, I killed a man I was supposed to heal. I couldn't save him, and now I'm going to face my fate when the villagers find out".

Maria eyes expanded in their sockets as she looked on in shock ."What a..re you talking about Miranda?" She asked so quietly, Miranda could barely make out the words.

"I said I killed a man". She replied whilst looking with teary big green eyes, at the brown grasses on the field surrounding their home.

Maria rushed over to her, taking her by the hand, she dragged her into the bedroom. " Tell me everything that happened ." she said.

Miranda recounted the events from start to finish. She told her how she had gone to administer herbs to the man following Lady Latisha's orders, and how the man had only gotten worse after taking the medicine.

Maria stood up from the bed and starting putting cloths in a basket. She arranged them meticulously as Miranda watched perplexed. "What are you doing mother?" She asked.

Maria stopped packing and looked up from the basket, "I know what you are capable of doing Miranda! I took care of you from childbirth, I watched you grow. Believe what you want, but I tell you, you're innocent, I won't let the people of Ponti misjudge you." She put her hands into her pocket and fetched out a silver necklace. "Take this with you child, go far away from here, run to Navyria there, you will find the answers you need."

Miranda looked from the necklace to Maria's face and back to the necklace. "I don't under..stand." She stuttered.

Maria smiled lovingly, "Go my child, if the fates concede we'll meet again." She pushed the basket into Miranda's hands and shoved her out the door. "I hear them coming, go now!"

Miranda started to reply, but Maria shut the door tightly at her face, She looked up and in a distance and saw the outline of people approaching at a steady pace, all shouting angrily.

Looking up at the sky, she realized that the night had come quickly, and the cold breeze was stingy. Beneath the silver moon Miranda ran away from everything she'd ever known.

Chapter 25

Lord Christopher was pissed.As he sat on his study chair, he reflected and tried to recall where he had gone wrong.

He looked at the shivering maid kneeling at his feet, the sight of her angered him more but he knew it wasn't her fault. His wife was as hard as a rock and as stubborn as a wild cat.

Christopher had never been this disoriented before, he had gone on a trip only to return and find out that his wife had left on the same night he was gone.

A sharp sniffle brought his wandering mind back to the situation at hand. He ordered the maid to get on her feet, He needed precise answers and she had better give it to him, or he won't hesitate to cut off her tongue.

"You said your mistress went on a trip alone. When was that and at what time.?"

Violet shoulders shook with fright. Her tiny form vibrated and she flinched at every move Lord Christopher made. She knew she was in trouble and the tiniest possibility of her leaving this room alive was nonexistent.

"My Lord, Lady Charlotte left the night you embarked on a journey to the wasted lands. She left at dusk because she didn't want anyone to recognize her, my Lord."Violet said, head still bent low.

Christopher watched the girl who looked stricken and ready to drop. He didn't have much time for such drama, so he went on to the next question."Where did she go? Why didn't she take the guards with her?" He queried.

" She headed for Ponti my Lord. Lady Charlotte demanded to go alone and when I offered to go with her she insisted that she go alone. I'm truly sorry my Lord." Violet couldn't stop the tears they just kept pouring.

Christopher listened with apt attention. He knew that Charlotte been in Ponti was for one reason, he couldn't help but feel the ache in his heart that his wife would keep such a great ordeal from him. He knew he was being hard on her, but he was going to make it right. He would go find her and support her because that was what he should have done from the start.

Looking at the young maid he took a sip from his crystal glass. He would have disposed of her for her inefficiency, but he didn't want to anger his wife. " You may leave, but remember this young woman. I only spare your life today because of the love I have for my wife. You should pray to your God, the next time may be your last."

Out of surprise, Violet's eyes bulged out of their sockets. Lord Christopher does not forgive easily, she quickly fell on her knees and thanked him, he only stood up from his chair, glass in hand, and left the room.

Lady Charlotte moved with spring. The old man had finally given answers to all her unanswered questions, she followed the route as he had directed. The excitement of seeing her daughter made her knees shake, would she like me? Would she look like Henry?Would she believe me?All these questions kept revolving in her mind.

A little commotion coming from afar, jutted her back to reality, she strained her eyes to see what was happening but all she saw was a large gathering of people.

Deciding to move on towards her destination she realized that the description the man had given her was just in front and her feet were leading her towards mayhem.

Lady Charlotte moved fast yet cautiously towards the gathering, she was not a fan of such meeting but she needed to know what was going on.

Chapter 26

A green bird with a black head and yellow wings flew past Miranda's right shoulder. The bird maneuvered its way through a dense bush and appeared at the other side. Perching on a fallen branch the bird seem to look like it was mocking her as it craned its neck to its left and looked on, in wonder.

A crestfallen Miranda, thought hard. She'd been in this bush for days, She hadn't any idea where to go, truth be told she was scared of what was waiting in front. She didn't know what the people of Navaria would look like, and much more, she hoped that the news of what she did would not be known by these people.

She placed a hand to shield her eyes from the scorching sun, she could barely see where she was going, she was sure that the energy from the sun could bake bread with little difficulties, how she wished she had brought some flour with her. She was that hungry.

Miranda jumped down from the miserly branch that was half way in the air, if she had to make it to Navaria tonight then she needed to move faster. It was best that she entered the city at night in order to keep attention and prying eyes away from her.

Moving towards the bird, it hopped backward, as it saw the still approaching form of Miranda, it stretched its yellow wings and flew into the sky, it gave a loud squeal and Miranda thought that it was a sign of approval. She was moving on.

After so many treacherous hours, Miranda saw the outskirts of the city as she stood on a hill. Unlike what she had heard, it wasn't that exciting, instead it looked gloomy, like a deep dark soulless place.

Miranda swallowed the lump that was forming in her throat, she didn't want to cry, she had to be strong for her self and for her mother. Picking up the hem of her dress, she began to descend the hill turgidly, she'd come too far to fall down, break a neck and die out here where no one would ever find her. The thought alone was depressing, but Miranda shoved it out of her mind, she had one place to be and that was Navaria. Mother had told her so.

Lady Charlotte couldn't believe what she was hearing, she felt her self falling but she wasn't hitting the ground. Her heart seem to pump at an inhuman speed, her lungs screamed for air but she wouldn't allow herself to breath. She should die, what fate was worst than loosing her own daughter once more, she had been so close.

Lady Charlotte looked menacingly at Maria Gonzalo, this was the woman who had stolen her day old child, she had thought of the various ways in which she would destroy her, but seeing her now on her knees, facing a crowd of people who wanted to kill her because of Miranda, Charlotte realized that she didn't have the strength to do all what she wished. She only prayed that her daughter be safe wherever she was.

The People of Ponti gathered around shouted and demanded that she bring out Miranda, but Maria was unshaken, she wouldn't speak. She raised her head, her hair was a mess from all the dragging and pulling, looking at the face of Charlotte Marcoti, Maria saw Miranda and more, She tried to subdue a smile at the striking resemblance.

Charlotte moved towards the woman, a woman she had sought for so long, she was angry, so angry. "Where is my daughter? She quietly asked despite the uproar.

Maria didn't know if she should ask first forgiveness or answer Charlotte's question. She opened her mouth to speak but no words were coming out, she could see the anticipation in Charlotte's dark blue eyes, the woman was still beautiful even though so much time had passed.

" Where is my daughter Maria Gonzalo? Tell me where she is, I beg you." Charlotte's voice shook, her eyes dangerous and wild.

Maria didn't know what to tell her, she opened her mouth to speak, and hesitated. "Miranda is safe My Lady, where she is, no one can reach her, but I assure you when the time is right you would find her."

Charlotte gritted her teeth so hard Maria was scared they would fall off. Her face was masked in agonizing anger. "I don't want to hear anymore nonsense! I want my child the one you so ruthlessly stole from me!" She whisper with urgency.

People began to draw nearer and the old man, who had talked to her in the market hours ago, stepped forward. He pointed at Maria, who was still on her knees.

"A decision have been made Maria. Since you've decided to keep a killer away from due punishment, you have been accorded to stand in for Miranda and thereby tomorrow at dusk, you will be hanged for harboring a killer and defying the laws of this land. This is our decision."

Lucy who had been in the crowd covered her mouth as a cry tore at her lips, she had seen all that happened, but she was so afraid to tell anyone, she couldn't keep quiet and let an innocent woman die. Miranda was innocent and so was her mother. She dashed out of the gathering and collapsed behind a house, there she wept painfully till a soft feminine voice broke through her subtle wailing.

"Why is such a pretty girl like you out her crying?"

Lucy cringed at been caught at her most private moment. She looked at the woman, surely she hadn't seen her around before.

"It was the only way I could let out my grief. Who are you?" She asked courageously.

Charlotte smiled at the girl's courageous stance. "My name is Charlotte and what should I call you?"

"I'm Lucy."

"A beautiful name." Charlotte said. She looked at the girl again and asked, "Are you in relation with the woman about to be executed?"

"Yes, she is my best friends mother.".

Charlotte's ears perked at the new information. "What was your friend like? Was she capable of what she had been accused of?".

Lucy paused for a moment, she didn't know how to reply, she knew the truth but she was so scared to tell, she looked at the woman and decided that she could trust her. There was this soft aura around her."No, Miranda is innocent, I saw it all, it was a set up. The herb that was needed to heal the man was poisoned."

Charlotte looked around and when she saw that no one was around she asked slowly to make sure. "Are you certain of this, Lucy?"

"Like I said, I saw it. Maria would be killed for something she knows nothing about." Lucy said unwavering.

Charlotte knew she had to do something, Maria had caused her pain, but she wouldn't want her to end like this, she had plans for her.

Chapter 27

Late at night when every creature was asleep, the hooves of horses galloped into Ponti. Christopher and his men had remained in the outskirt of the village till night fall, as soon as the darkness filled the land, they rode in.

Christopher looked at the little houses, they looked so tiny and uncomfortable to live in. Waving a hand to signal his men, the five of them stopped as they saw his raised hands. The first man moved his horse closer to Lord Christopher, he bent his head to listen to what he had to say, "What is the problem my Lord?" He asked quizzically.

Looking at the surrounding, he turned his head both ways, he didn't know why he felt that something was terrible wrong. Brushing away the dreadful feeling, he whispered into the ear of the man, "I don't have a good feeling about this place Gabriel, I want you all to disperse, it will be more easier to find Lady Charlotte that way and leave here immediately."

Gabriel nodded his head in understanding, "okay my Lord, we'll do just as you've ordered."Lord Christopher tilted his head, and moved his horse forward, quietly. He listened for movements all around, he couldn't possibly guess where she could be at this time. He looked towards the cheap building where travellers dwelled after a long trip, one of his men was already approaching the building, He hoped that she was in there.

Charlotte stood up from the scantily dressed bed that she had been pretending to sleep on, she picked her cape and wore it over her head. Picking up the lantern that was sitting idle on a stool, she found her sandals and wore them quietly.

She opened the door and ventured into the pitch dark night, dimming her lantern flames to draw less attention to her presence she moved stealthy towards Maria's holding cell, just as lord Christopher's soldier reached the building.

On reaching there the guard positioned at the door was sleeping, the loud snore emanating from his nostrils could wake up an entire village, but ironically, she was the only one awake. She put off the flames and dropped the lantern on the ground, moving one foot at a time, Charlotte reached the still sleeping guard.

She saw a set of keys sticking out of his pockets, she stretched a hand to pick it up but the guard rolled to the other side. Biting her lips to help keep her temper in check, she moved to the opposite direction and saw that the key was almost falling off. Taking a deep breath, she reached for the key and when she finally pulled it and felt the metal lying on her palm, she grinned.

Maria looked at the dark night through the little opening around the cabin, in which she had been kept. It was going to be her last night on earth, she thought of all the events that had taken place in her life, some significant and some, not so significant.

As she thought about Miranda and where she could be, the sound of the door opening brought her thoughts to a halt. Was it time already? She let out a shaky breath, death was indeed terrifying. The thought shook her to her marrows.

The person standing behind her moved softly, why was the guard moving quietly? Maria thought. She began to hyperventilate as she thought of all the things that could possibly go wrong, maybe he was here to molest her! Frantically she turned towards the door and the non smiling face of Lady Charlotte came into view.

Charlotte just stood by the already closed door and watched as different emotions played on Maria's face, she indeed had looked terrified, then surprised and now confused. Maria's lips moved as she attempted to say something, but Charlotte placed a slender finger on her lips,indicating that she kept quiet, Maria nodded uncertainly. Lady Charlotte produced the bunch of keys, and tried each one on Maria's bounded fists, "Don't consider me your saviour Maria, I'm your worst night mare." Charlotte told her as the lock finally clicked open.Maria didn't know how to respond so she Just nodded her head in understanding. "Good, now let's go before the guard wakes up." Lady Charlotte whispered.

Maria and Charlotte ran as fast as they could through the Forest part, the plan was to leave Ponti before dawn. As the two ran, they avoided the road as much as possible not wanting to get caught. Taking another turn, Maria first heard it, she stopped running as she called lady Charlotte's attention. "My Lady, I hear the sounds of hooves." She whispered.

Charlotte stopped and listened and it was the unmistakable sound of horses approaching, she turned to maria. " Quickly hide!"Both women ducked behind bushes as the horses kept on approaching at a steady pace. "Do you think they've found out about my disappearance?"Maria asked in the dark. "How would I know? You're the wanted one here so keep quiet, I don't want them finding us." Charlotte replied.

Maria nodded even though Charlotte couldn't see her, it was that dark. The horses passed through their hiding place, immediately they were gone, the two women ran out of the bush.

•••Christopher kept a fair distance away from his men, they had reunited after the search and Lady Charlotte was still nowhere to be found. As soon as he took a bend, the shape of two women came running and that startled his horse, he quickly jumped down from the horse and picked up the one who had fallen down. As he picked her up, he saw her face and he squeaked in surprise.

"Charlotte!"

"Christopher what are you doing here?" Charlotte asked perplexed.

" I came to find you, oh thank goodness you're fine." He turned to her companion, "who is she? She's certainly not your daughter."

Charlotte took a side ways glance at her. "Christopher this woman is Maria Gonzalo, and we need to leave Ponti now. Our lives are in danger."

Christopher pushed on, "where's your daughter? Isn't she the reason why you came here?"

"There's no time to answer your questions, I'll answer them all, once we reach Navaria."Christopher nodded and whistled for his men.

The group left Ponti quietly, filled with apprehension.

Chapter 28

The different bodies clustered together made Miranda dizzy, she pushed through the mass of people as she tried to find a place to stay for a while, it was indeed a strange place with strange people.When she remembered the stories she had heard about Navria, she wondered why anyone would want to come here, it was stripped of off the beauty of nature and it looked uneventful.

Pushing the disturbing thought out of her mind, Miranda finally noticed the little inn at the end of a shabby street. She clambered over excitedly, as she knocked at the door, a wrinkling old woman appeared and poked her head out just a bit. "How may I help you, young woman?" The woman asked with her mouth open, exposing brown cracked teeth.

Miranda's smile fell from her lips immediately she met the woman's unfriendly gaze."Good morning madam.

My name is Miranda and I'm new in town, I am in search of an inn to stay for a while. Do you have any room available please?"

The woman looked at her from the dirty tips of her shoes to her uncombed hair. "I'm sorry young woman, but we don't have anymore rooms please go away." She moved to push the door close, but Miranda stopped her.

"Please I beg you, if you can be of help, I will be forever grateful. I have no where to go." She deep her hand into her side pocket in a frenzy and fetched out a handful of coins, "look I have enough money to pay for the room, don't be discouraged by my torn dress."

The woman with pity in her eyes, shook her head slowly. "I can't help you, be on your way, I can't risk the lives of people in here. If you say you just came into town then its possible that you've been infected already."

Miranda looked at the woman with uncertainty and wonder, she raised her hand to call the woman's atten-tion, but the door was already closed. What does she mean by infected already?

She faced the opposite direction and started the walk aimlessly around. Seeing a fruit vendor she approached the woman's table and purchased a few Apples and grapes, she decided that she'd eat them first then think of what to do next. The woman handed her the bag of fruits and she thanked her as she placed a few coins on her palm. She brought the shimmering juicy apple to her lips, and took a hearty bite.

From across the street a loud wail was heard, Miranda looked at the direction in which the voice was coming from, a little girl was sprawled out on the floor and there appeared to be a cut on her knee. She dashed to the child's side who was bleeding profusely.

Miranda scanned the place looking for no one in particular, she turned to face the crying child, "Who's your mother?" As soon as she asked, an elegant looking man ran out of the tailor shop from across the street.He appeared at the child's side in no time, his face was contoured in anger, "Belinda! Why in God's name did you leave the store?" He bellowed.

Miranda looked at the man discreetly, he wore a white shirt and dark pants, he looked very handsome. She blushed and stood up from her sprawled out position on the floor. Her movement drew John Walker's attention to her, he took one look at the girl, she looked terrible, he attempted to act nice. "And who are you?" He asked with a nice smile, showing his perfect teeth.

From that moment Miranda knew her life was going to change forever..

Chapter 29

Argo looked at the face of his Master with fear sipping out of his pores. He had remembered his masters instruction clearly the day he was released, find the girl and find the girl, he didn't have any other option. Now here he stood, not only had he lost the girl he had also lost the only person who could tell them where Miranda was.He knew today was going to be his last day on earth and he only wished that some sort of intervention would keep him from his fate.

Magnus sat still on his chair, his hands which were placed on the desk trembled but he didn't let His emotions show in his face. He looked up at the excuse of a man standing before him and said,"So Maria and the girl are both missing, you say?"

Argo swallowed   a large portion of thick lump that had saturated in his throat. "My Lord my accomplice in

Ponti tells me that both Maria and Miranda, have left the village."

Placing his hand on his chin he looked on at the trembling man, Argo raised his eyes to that of Magnus and as quickly as he did, he cast them down, he was so afraid to die, but he would have ended the life of another without a seconds breath. How ironic.Master Magnus stood dainty on his feet, he moved towards the wine cabinet and fetched out a bottle of expensive wine, carrying g two glasses, he place one in the table and handed the other to Argo. Pouring them both a drink, he asked Argo to drink because it was a beautiful evening.

Placing the thick glass in his mouth, he didn't see the last piece of foamy substance dissolve into the wine, he drank it sceptically and yet with a hint of pride, no one has tasted from the master's wine collection, he was the first and unknown to him, it was going to be the last.

Miranda watched the sleeping child and her lips stretched in a half smile she looked just adorable. Her hair a wavy ebony black was sprawled out on the pillow and her lips were puckered like she had something to say in her sleep. Miranda inspected the bandage that she'd placed on her injured knee, it looked fine, taking the blanket, she placed it over the child's body.

After the incident on the street she had insisted to attend to Belinda, John had refuted the idea and had asked her to go home but she had insisted, so here she was in this pink spacious room, bigger than the house that she had lived in all her life.

As she smiled at the memory, a thin knock penetrated her thoughts and the door to Belinda's room opened. A woman in an elegant silver gown glided towards the sleeping child, Miranda took one look at the woman and realised that the woman wasn't even aware of her presence in the room. The woman stroked the girl's hair which looked just like hers and whispered sweet words into her ears, as she pecks her on her little head, she finally noticed another presence in the room. She spoke without turning."I'm Lady Henrietta, who are you?" She asked with her hands still stroking the child's hair.

Miranda out of courtesy, bowed her head as she responded, "my name is Miranda Gonzalo, I attended to little Belinda's injury." She didn't want to say the word *daughter * for she wasn't certain yet, Although the resemblance was glaring enough.

Henrietta smiled, still without looking at her, "you have a very beautiful name Miranda, and from the sound of your voice I can also tell that you're beautiful. You don't have to be afraid to speak, I heard the hesitation in your voice Miranda, this little girl is my daughter and also the young man who brought you here is my son. I say thank you for what you've done, now if you'll please allow me to ask, I'll like to know how much your services cost."

Miranda stood mouth agape, she had insisted to help Belinda not because of any reward but because she wanted to, She opted to apologize and tell the Lady that she couldn't collect any fee. "I'm sorry lady Henrietta, I can't take any money from you, what I did for Belinda, I did for love. Don't look at my poor state and judge me by it." As she said those words, lady Henrietta finally turned towards her direction and as she did, Miranda placed a hand over her mouth to hold the surprised squeal that tried to break free.

Lady Henrietta's eyes stared unseeing, "I do not see your poor state Miranda, what I offered you was the right thing to do. If you do not want instant payment then we could arrange something, as you can see now that my little girl is ill, She will need someone to stay with her, she's only 9 and there's a lot that she needs to learn and I can't teach her everything and neither can John. ".

Lady Henrietta stood speaking for a second and took a deep breath, " if you are willing Miranda Gonzalo, will you be Belinda's nanny?"

Miranda's entire body went rigid as the word stumbled out of the woman's mouth. She sucked in a deep breath as she looked at the fragile girl in the bed. "I'm no nanny, I haven't taken care of children before, I'll do a very bad job and I don't want to use your wonderful daughter as an example." She finished with a solid shake of her head forgetting that lady Henrietta was blind.

"I'll give you the night to think about it, the guest room had been prepared for you, by tomorrow I will be waiting for a reply." The woman kissed the little girl one more time and move softly out of the room.

Miranda moved over to the bed and picked Belinda's tiny hands placing them on her palm as she thought. I am good with medicine and not children! Where do I start from?

Chapter 30

Lady Charlotte lay curled up on her gigantic bed. She hadn't left her room since two days after they returned from Ponti, Christopher had visited her everyday but he ended up leaving disappointed as Charlotte wouldn't say anything to him. As days went by, things became more difficult for them both, Charlotte couldn't get over the truth that she had lost her daughter again.

Maria had been locked up in the dungeon, she was given food and fresh clothing twice a day. Other inmates started to whisper and soon enough it became a demand, they wanted to know why Maria gets better treatment and attention than them. Maria would sit in her cell and watch them as they screamed for answers.She didn't understand why lady Charlotte would spare her life after what she had done in the past, only to end up locking her in this place. She felt miserable but she was ready to accept her punishment.

Three months had passed and everyday was eventful for Miranda, she had learnt what she needed to do for Belinda. They both engaged in different activities together, Miranda taught her how to weave baskets and Belinda was really improving everyday.

After she accepted the offer from lady Henrietta, she had a tough time trying to learn the roles of how things worked. The first few weeks were terrible for both her and the child, sometimes she'd say something and realize that what she had just spoken was not for a little girls hearing.

Often, Belinda would want to be left alone, but Miranda never knew when to take the hint, till one bright morning when Belinda was sulking and Miranda thought it wise to try and cheer her up.

"Belinda sweetie, please get up" Belinda turned towards the opposite direction, showing Miranda her b ack.Miranda tried again, "Belinda I want you to get up this minute!, breakfast is ready and you can't stay right here when you should be downstairs eating.

Belinda had sprung up from the bed with tears in her eyes and ran out of the house, Miranda went to look for her but she couldn't find her, getting nervous because of the girls disappearance, she rushed to girl's brother's office and knocked loudly.

Since she came to live with the Walker's she had spoken to Master John just once, not that she was scared of him but she automatically turned into an idiot whenever she was around him, so she figured it was best if she didn't say anything when he was around.

Knocking loudly the second time, she heard a low grunt coming from the inside of the room, taking it as a yes, she opened the door and walked in.John was standing by the window staring at the grasses, he turned to her and smiled thinly, he usually does that whenever he saw her, Miranda had noticed." Good morning master John ". She greeted with her head bent low.

", John, just call me john" he corrected as he put his hand in his pant pocket.

" okay John". Miranda blushed a little, "I'm here because of Belinda."

At the mention of his sisters name he perked up, "what seem to be the problem?" He asked, a frown creasing his forehead.

"She ran out of bed this morning after I asked her to come down for breakfast, she didn't return so I went to look for her and I didn't find her."

John moved over to Miranda, he touched her shoulders softly as he looked into her eyes, " have you checked the meadow?"

Miranda shook her head," what would she be doing in there? " she asked agitated.

"Miranda listen, my father was my sisters hero and after he died she became withdrawn even if we all thought that she was too young to understand death. She wouldn't talk to anyone and when she feels sad, she goes to his graveside."

Miranda nodded in understanding, "I'll go check on her now. Thank you mas... John" she said quietly, still finding it hard to call him by name.

"Miranda?" John called after her,

"yes John."

"Give her time, she'll come around, believe me.

She nodded visibly and left the room. That was the second time she had a conversation with him, and from that day onward Belinda opened up to her and the two became so close.

Henrietta would hear their laughter whenever they were around her and her heart would soar, finally some-one else could make her daughter happy.

Chapter 31

Lord Christopher stumbled for the fourth time, he grunted as he held unto the railing, what was going on? He wondered. He had been feeling weak in his bones lately, last night he couldn't sleep for he was so hot and feverish. Taking an already soiled handkerchief from his pocket he coughed strong and deep into it, as he brought it away from his mouth his tired eyes scanned the surface and he saw a reasonable amount of blood on it.

Christopher knew he had caught the disease and he shook with dread, standing straight he ambled to his room he knew he didn't have much longer in a few days he would die. The thought was like a needle pricking his heart. He moved blindly in search for his room, he didn't know if he should tell his wife or not he didn't want her to breakdown more than she had already.

On finally reaching his door he went straight to his window and stared at the beauty of the evening, as he started on, he heard a knock on his door.

"Who is there? He asked softlyThe maid behind the door replied timidly." Lord Christopher dinner has been served."   Christopher moved to open the door, he looked at the smallish girl before him, she looked so young and fragile, and very much frightened."thank you for coming up to inform me about dinner, but I wouldn't be going down because I would like to be left alone. Tell your mistress what I have just told you."

The maid bowed quickly and took a U turn back downstairs, as she walked fast she turned subtly and saw from the slightly opened door as Lord Christopher held his midsection as he stumbled back into his room.

As days went by Miranda tried to put the event that had taken place in Ponti at the back of her mind and focus on the present but anytime she came in contact with plants she felt the chill as it ran down her spine.

One early morning she was leaving the house for the market, the pantry was half empty and the rain was coming , it was unwise not to have enough food in the house before the rain starts. As she past the stairs she overheard two cleaners discussing about a very deadly disease that was infecting people, she feigned to not pay attention and was about to walk past them when the redhead Lucida called out to her.

"Hey there Miranda, I hear you got your way into this manor because of your healing abilities?". Miranda speared her a glance as the memories came splashing back like waves in a storm and offered a quick smile as she replied, " I am no longer in the business of healing, Lucida."

Lucida cocked a brow enquiringly, "what say then, was your reason for leaving medicine? It is truly a befitting occupation, much better than babysitting," she conclud-ed with spite.

Miranda having had enough of her ramble, picked up her basket and descended down the stairs as Lucida spoke fervently and with so much anger."You better use your skills witch! People are dying and a self-centered person like you wouldn't do anything 'bout it."Miranda let her feet lead her to the backdoor and straight to the market.

Chapter 32

The rain came and so did so many ailments, from common cold to pneumonia and lastly the epidemic that has swiftly contributed in the dwindling of residents of Navaria and their neighbouring cities alike. Henrietta had received the letter on Thursday which Miranda had read to her on that fateful evening.

She hadn't been in good relations with her deceased brother's first wife so imagine the surprise when she was brought a letter and a very desperate one, even though she was blind she could listen and the words she heard held hidden pleas.

Lady Charlotte had been specific in her letter, she was in need of a good doctor who could heal her husband for he was dying. He had been suffering for eight months and she only got to find out two months ago that he had been infected. She wrote that she had been so unobservant because of related issues which Henrietta was no stranger to, as the missing child is her niece. She ended with a plea that if perhaps by chance she comes across a healer, "send them my way, and I will be internally grateful ".

Henrietta listened as the letter came to an end. She took Miranda's hand as she thanked her." No need to thank me Madam Henrietta, it was my pleasure reading to you."

Henrietta smiled and Miranda couldn't help but smile too. " Well child, since you have read me the letter I see no point in keeping the story away from you."Miranda objected, saying that it was a personal family issue but Henrietta reminded her that she was part of the family and therefore she should listen. She gave in.

Henrietta was born on a cold July night, her parents had been delighted to have had her. Years past and her mother kept trying for another child hopefully a son, five years later Henry was born. Everyone was jubilant. Henry was an heir and therefore he had every training he needed.

Years Past like a bad storm and in one of those terrible year Henrietta lost her sight. She was a sick child, and as such the two brother and sister were inseparable, soon Henrietta was married to Lord Brighton and Henry watched his sister go away to start her family. Soon enough their father died in his sleep and Henry became

Lord, he was reminded that as a ruler he needed a lady and so he began the search for a wife.

Months past and finally in a Ball organised by his mother, he met lady Charlotte. She was an interesting woman and soon enough he found out that he wanted to spend the rest of the night with her in his arms, dancing under the crystal balls, and thereafter the rest of their lives together.

Things were looking good for Henry, his wife was heavy with child and no one was as happy as him. Two months to the time of Charlotte's childbirth, Henry was killed in an ambush. The baby was born and lost, five years later Charlotte remarried. Henrietta had licked her wounds and till this day she had never forgotten nor forgiven Charlotte.

Miranda sat still as she digested the story, it was a long one with so many twist, anguish, love, pain. Miranda hugged her and left the room quietly, at the time she closed the bedroom door, Henrietta was still sitting in the same exact position.

That night Miranda toss from one end to another she couldn't sleep, she woke up several times and pondered on what to do concerning the letter she had read. She felt a need to reach out to this woman and help her, she might have to go against Henrietta's wish but she had to do something, or that poor man would pay the price for a feud that had lasted two decades.

Chapter 33

It was in the early hours of the next day that Miranda made up her mind, she was going to help Lady Charlotte's dying husband. Lucida was right, it was time for her to face her fears heads on. She remembered Maria and a tear slipped down her soft cheek.

When Henrietta learned about Miranda's motives she advised her to stay away from that family, because all they did was hurt people, Miranda smiled and assured her. "Lady Henrietta, I will certainly stay out of trouble." So the next day a carriage was prepared for Miranda , she held a crying Belinda and made promises to return the next week.

They watched her as she rode out of the mansion, to begin another mission.

She arrived at Lord Christopher's massive mansion without any incident. Miranda was awed at how big and prosperous his lands looked. At the far end of the land she saw the animals grazing and boy where they large! She concluded then that he was a very influential man.

Her carriage driver helped her with her baggage and soon she was led into the mansion by a very pleasant servant with a nice accent. Miranda knew she was going to enjoy her stay here, but first things first she needed to see the sick patient. She excused the nice servant whom had assisted her at the door and asked him to take her to the Lord of the mansion, he had declined, telling her that Lady Charlotte had ordered him to make her a bath and make sure she ate some food as she must be tired.

The older male servant didn't look like one who was going to give into any argument Miranda was gently brewing in her mind, so she had quietly behaved and accepted but inwardly planned to have a quick bath. She wasn't here for the good food or best treatment, a dying man needed her attention.

Dinner was amazing, she hadn't seen so much food before and the mere sight of it made her dizzy she felt bad that she had forgotten Henrietta's fine cooking, but she straightened up and had a small portion. Later that night, she met lord Christopher he looked pale and his eyes were sunken, she adjusted the blanket down to his torso and checked his heartbeat it was quiet in there, for a second fear gripped her until she heard the soft but slow beating of his heart.

He didn't have much strength left, he was so weak and looked half dead. Miranda mixed an energy drink for him and he gulped it happily, she could tell that he was hanging on to the thin thread of life he had left. Next she mixed her first batch of healing herb, he drank it and in no time he was sound asleep. She covered his body carefully and left the room.

As she reached the hall way, she realized that she didn't know whether to go left or right. It was late and she didn't want to startle anyone with her movements, she took the left and walked quietly down the hall, as she moved in the darkness she sighted a figure standing at the balcony, she ncreased her steps, finally someone she could ask for directions!

She approached the person who still hadn't looked at her, "hello, good evening, I am the new healer attending to Lord Christopher, please can you show me the way to my room?"The woman turned and offered a thin smile, although it was dark Miranda could see that the smile didn't reach her eyes. "Hello healer, I am Lady Charlotte and your room is the other way."

Miranda couldn't hide her amazement, the woman was beautiful and her attire elegant, she thanked her for her kindness and took the hallway back to her room. As she walked she kept turning back and looking at the woman, she didn't ask about her husband's health which many women would have done.

Chapter 34

Lord Christopher had made great improvement since the healer came around, she was truly gifted at least that was what everyone thought. Lady Charlotte picked up a piece of cucumber from the silver tray, she chewed slowly as she watched her husband sleep peacefully for the first time in almost a year. She hadn't seen much of the healer after their encounter the first night and she hadn't cared, but she felt it was time to say a proper hello to the girl and of course, she was going to be paid handsomely for doing a good job.

Miranda was mixing the last medicine that she would give to Lord Christopher when he wakes up. It was the herb she had mixed a year ago in Ponti, she was sure it was going to make a remarkable change in Lord Christopher's health but she didn't know what exactly. Putting the last of the ingredient in, she rose up to discard the leafs when a young lad ran up to her.

"Excuse me ma'm," Miranda replied with a hello as the young man began to talk." Lady Charlotte has requested that you check the health condition of the prisoners held in the dungeon". Miranda was taken aback by the request and asked quietly. "Why me? I didn't come here for that, I am in this place because of lord Christopher and lord Christopher alone."

The boys face flushed red as he tried to relax and explain to her but Miranda didn't let him talk as she continued,"I am sorry to be directing questions at you, I will go to the dungeon but only after I have administered this herb to lord Christopher, he should be up any minute."

The boy breathed a sign of relief as he thanked her and ran off, apparently to deliver another message. Miranda packed the herb and headed upstairs to change out of her soiled cloths. As she wore a green cotton gown,she looked at herself in the mirror and smiled it was beautiful, she sighted the silver necklace that Maria had given to her, if she was going to do something remarkable today then she wanted to do it with that necklace. As she reached for it she heard a knock on her door, forgetting all about her necklace she opened the door, Lady Charlotte's beautiful face came into view.

Lady Charlotte stood still as she swam deeper into those green pool which were Miranda's eyes, she tried to speak but nothing was coming out, she remembered those eyes clearly yet she was a bit confused. She cleared her throat and spoke, "Hello my dear, I came to thank you for what you have done for my husband, and I apologise for not informing you myself about the prisoners. I haven't been very much available please forgive my absence."

Miranda was touched by the lady's calm and polite nature, she smiled and shook her head. "There is no problem my Lady, in fact I was just about to give lord Christopher his last herb, you may join me if you wish ."Charlotte smiled and led the way as Miranda exited the room and closed the door behind her, the silver necklace sat idly on the table, forgotten.

Chapter 35

After she finished with Lord Christopher she monitored him for an hour and when she saw that everything was going fine she picked up her little bag and headed for the dungeon. The road that led there was dark and depressing, she wondered why someone as kindhearted as lady Charlotte would keep a human being in such a place, nobody deserves to live like this no matter the graveness of their crimes.

She mounted the steps and descended lower into the darkness, as she felt like going back because of how edgy she was then she sighted a guard standing just outside a gate, approaching him she informed him of her purpose here and he opened the gate without further questions.

She thought she had seen worse, but this place was hell on earth, it reeked of urine and the stench got her clutching her nose together unintentionally. She found a somewhat clean spot and deposited her herbs there, she began to mix them diligently. She wanted every person here to feel healthy even if the effect of the herb wouldn't last a week, the place was just too dirty and unkept!

After twenty minutes she began to move from one holding cell to another, some men called her stinky names, other shouted that she should; come closer and they would show her how to have a good time". She ignored them all and made her way deeper into the place, she was determined.

On reaching a particular cell the place looked a little clean and it wasn't smelly like the others she had passed, she craned her neck to see the occupant of the cell but the woman was facing the wall, she let her hands knock the gate but the woman inside didn't budge. Miranda was getting anxious so she called out the the woman. " Hello lady, please turn towards this direction, I don't have all day come forward and take your herb, it will make you feel better, I promise you."

Maria Gonzalo froze at the voice she just heard. She didn't know what to feel, she smiled a little then tears sprang from both her eyes. Turning slowly she saw who she thought she would never again. Miranda was just as shocked as Maria, she stuttered as she tried to talk

. "Mother? Wh...at are you do..ing here in this filthy place!"

Maria couldn't control herself, the tears just kept coming, Miranda quickly reached for her hands and squeezed them, "I am going to get you out of here, I trust lady Charlotte will be so kind and let you out."Maria tried to talk but Miranda was already out of the door. She slid down and prayed that Miranda forgave her, then she counted the minutes.

Chapter 36

Lady Charlotte was in her study room when the guard came in with a message, she asked him to let in the healer and also fetch her a bag of gold, he left after ushering a dishevelled Miranda in. Lady Charlotte was a woman who loved minding her business but the state in which she saw the young girl standing before her made her curious. "What can I do for you young lady?" She asked. Miranda who was still breathing heavily due to fatigue made a noise and lady Charlotte knew she needed a drink of water. She gave her a glass.

After gulping down the water and successfully spilling half of it on herself Miranda was ready to talk. "With all due respect my Lady, I have come to discuss a serious matter."Lady Charlotte smiled softly like a mother would do to a doting child. "Is this meeting about your pay? don't worry, I just sent for your reward."

"No my Lady, that is the problem I don't want gold nor silver, I want something else in return."

At this point lady Charlotte's was sceptical. " what do you want then? Land? property? Just name it."

Miranda shook her head vehemently. "I want the release of my mother in place of your reward."Lady Charlotte's eyes were wide as saucers, I have your mother in my dungeon? How come I didn't recognize you. Who exactly is your mother?"

Miranda answered softly, "My mother is Maria Gonzalez and my name is Miranda." Lady Charlotte backed away from her desk as Miranda continued to plead, "please let her go, whatever she had done I know she feels sorry."

Charlotte's couldn't hear a word of what Miranda was saying all she saw was her long lost daughter of twenty and one. "You're just so beautiful like your father." That seemed to shut Miranda up as she asked with zeal, "you know my father? Please where can I find him? I have never met him because mother wouldn't tell me anything."

Charlotte's already broken heart cracked ones more as Miranda gave her motherly title to another. She screamed for the guards and asked them to fetch Maria Gonzalez .

As they waited for the third party Lady Charlotte couldn't take her eyes off her daughter, she had sparkling eyes like her father and long brown hair just like hers, she saw Henry and Charlotte in this perfect being sitting right in front of her. Several times Miranda caught her staring and she did nothing to hide it, who could blame her? She hadn't seen her child in twenty one years.

The door to the study came open and Maria was escorted in, at the sight of her, Miranda sprang to her feet and collapsed on her body all the while crying soundly. Lady Charlotte watched them from her desk her own eyes welling up with tears.

After the moment passed Maria cleared her throat and began to talk. "Miranda, I know this would come as a blow to you but I have to tell you the truth."

Miranda moved in her seat as she inquired curiously, "what truth mother? What is it that you have to tell me? I know you just saw sunlight after a long time, but don't worry I will mix you a herb to..."

"Stop! " Maria said with finality, "listen to what I have to tell you and what I say is the truth. I have lied to you from birth, Miranda I am not your mother. When you were born I was an accomplice with a very evil man who wanted you, on getting to the place where I was to deliver you to him I couldn't do it, and so I ran away with you to Ponti. We stayed there and I told the villagers that you were my daughter and I your mother."

Miranda stood up from the seat, she looked from maria to Charlotte and then back to Maria, "who then is my mother?" She asked because she already knew the truth. Crying softly Maria replied admist tear, "Lady Charlotte is your birth mother, I took you away from her. I am so sorry."

Miranda looked at Charlotte and they held their gaze, she saw herself in her mother and she felt the pain she had felt all these years. Lady Charlotte's extended hand brought Miranda out of her reverie, she couldn't accept anything right now she needed time to think, so she turned and walked out the door.

Chapter 37

Miranda was hurting, she felt betrayed but she didn't let that consume her, she checked on Lord Christopher everyday till the man could sit, eat and walk around without aid.

She was absorbed in her work and didn't pay anyone any mind but she knew that she had to talk to her mother, the woman was hurting more than she was.

That noon she visited her biological mother in her chamber, Lady Charlotte wasn't expecting her and the surprise was a good one.

They talked about everything and anything, Miranda felt the connection and so did Charlotte. Lady Charlotte told her about her father , how they met, fell In love and started a family and finally how he died. Miranda wept a little but held her mother tight.

Miranda refused to talk about Maria it was a topic she didn't want to touch just yet, she didn't trust herself to make the right decision. Lady Charlotte knew better than to bring it up, all she wanted was to hold her child.

Magnus sat in his lair and all be could think of was the gentle face of Cara, Augustus daughter. She was so young and tender and he wanted to have her. He wobbled down to her little room where she slept every night, he opened the door and Saw her sleeping form.

The candles were shinning bright and she looked so beautiful, Magnus undid his pants and crawled over her. Cara felt the bed dip and held her breath, she didn't know who was in her room but the twelve year old knew that the intruder wasn't here for a chat.

She let him settle on the bed and as he played with her hair she summoned courage and Jumped out of the bed, as she did she threw the covers on him and in the process knocked down the candles. The beddings immediately caught fire and she ran out of the room while locking the door behind her.

Magnus screamed and shouted for help but no one came running because he had given them orders not to disturb.

His charred body was discovered under the debris, little Cara was searched for, but never found.

Chapter 38

After a week of having a blissful family reunion Miranda invited Henrietta, John and Belinda over. Henrietta almost turned down the request but because of Miranda pleas she agreed.

The guest arrived and they were welcomed, Lady Charlotte smiled and even acknowledged Henrietta.

When the meal have been served and everyone was filled to the brim, Lady Charlotte broke the news.

"Everyone seated at the table, I present to you my long lost daughter Miranda!"

Henrietta was ecstatic as she hugged her niece for a long time. Belinda smile widened and she hugged her nanny now turned cousin tight. John was the last to make a comment, he looked closely at Miranda then he said.

"Turns out we are family after all Miranda, welcome to the family once again."

The drinking and merriment continued as lady Charlotte gave them the detail of what happened.

When all seem quiet in the house Lady Charlotte approached Henrietta who was standing at the balcony. "I know you are there Charlotte, you should be sleeping peacefully now that you've found your daughter, why then are you awake?"

Charlotte shook her he'd dramatically even though she knew that Henrietta couldn't see her. "I am here to talk about us, and give reasons why we should put the past behind us."

Henrietta drew her cloth closer to her body, she suddenly felt cold, Charlotte continued. "We have a new addition to the family now and she would need support from us both, if we keep on fighting and disagreeing she would be caught in the crossfire."

Henrietta took a deep breath, "I agree with you, she's our responsibility now and we need to set aside our differences. My brother would have wanted that of me."

She turned eyes unseeing and said.

"Let's bury the hatchet Charlotte, but mind you, I am doing this for the sake of my niece."

It had   been three weeks since anyone talked about Maria, that morning the family all sat down and Miranda was the center of attention.

She told them how life in Ponti had been and how Maria had been a good mother to her even if she had lied.

Maria had taught her a lot and she would forever be grateful to her. As she was talking , Maria entered the room quietly.

Lady Charlotte looked at the woman who had made her cry, made her sleepless and depressed. "Maria, I would say, so nice to meet you but this isn't the case."

Maria bowed her head and spoke softly. "I do understand your anger my lady and I have come to apologise to you and every member of this family that I have hurt."

Miranda moved to her side and hugged her, then she whispered. "You did what you felt was right at that time mother, you saved my life and I am grateful for that. We all have forgiven you so don't fret."

With tears in her eyes she thanked them for accepting her, everyone hugged her as a sign of forgiveness, even lady Charlotte although she was hesitant.

That night Maria fled from Navaria, she needed to start again and this time she was going to do the right things.

Epilogue

Miranda and lord Christopher watched as the stallion took its first breath of nature. The mother horse lay tiredly as the stallion struggled for milk. Miranda was the first to speak, "isn't this sight beautiful father! I feel reborn."Christopher smiled as he took her hand and they continued on their way, ",I never got the chance to properly thank you for saving me." He said.

Miranda was having none of it, she frowned and said quickly,

"father, daughters don't let their fathers die. So enough with the appreciation, all thanks should go to Maria, she made me pursue my dreams and sacrificed everything for my safety." She took a pause and continued. "It was quiet unfortunate that she didn't stay."

"Yes". Christopher chipped in, " but as long as I live she will forever be in my heart . Come on let's rush over I bet lunch is served already."

Miranda smiled all the way back to the Mansion. She couldn't wait to get back to her mother, she smiled at her stepfather and he smiled down at her.

The sky was a bright orange colour, it was a good day.